HANK ZIPZER

The Mostly True Confessions of the World's Best Underachiever

DAY OF THE IGUANA

by Henry Winkler and Lin Oliver

HANK ZIPZER

The Mostly True Confessions of the
World's Best Underachiever

DAY OF THE IGUANA

Grosset & Dunlap • New York

Text copyright © 2003 by Fair Dinkum and Lin Oliver Productions, Inc. Illustrations copyright © 2003 by Grosset & Dunlap. All rights reserved. Published by Grosset & Dunlap, a division of Penguin Young Readers Group, 345 Hudson Street, New York, NY, 10014. GROSSET & DUNLAP is a trademark of Penguin Group (USA) Inc. Published simultaneously in Canada. Printed in the U.S.A.

Library of Congress Cataloging-in-Publication Data is available.

ISBN 0-448-43212-9 (pbk)   A B C D E F G H I J

ISBN 0-448-43288-9 (hc)   A B C D E F G H I J

To my wife Stacey who taught me the meaning of true courage and inner power.—H.W.

CHAPTER 1

"I HAVE GREAT NEWS," I said. "Charlie the Clown has diarrhea."

My best friend, Frankie Townsend, looked at me like my brain had just flopped out of my head and turned into mashed potatoes.

"Hey, man, that *is* super news," Frankie said, rolling his eyes. "It's always cool to hear about a clown with stomach problems."

Ashley Wong, my other best friend, burst out laughing and fell down onto the old couch that we use for meetings in our clubhouse. Our clubhouse is a storage room in the basement of our apartment building.

"Go ahead and laugh, Ashweena," I said to her. "But you won't be laughing when you hear that there's money in this for us."

Ashley stopped laughing immediately, like I knew she would. She is the business manager for Magik 3, which is the magic group we started a couple of months ago. We've performed two times for real money. Frankie is the magician, and he's a great one, too. I'm the magician's assistant and all-around idea man. Ashley is really good at the money part, which makes me happy because I don't understand money or change or anything like that.

"Talk to me, Hank," Ashley said. "I'm hearing a business opportunity."

"My Aunt Maxine is throwing a birthday party this weekend for my three-year-old twin cousins, Jake and Zack," I began. "Charlie the Clown was supposed to perform. But it turns out he ate some bad clams at Luigi's Oyster house. Now he's got—"

"Diarrhea," Frankie and Ashley chimed in, stifling a laugh.

"Right. And he can't do the party."

"And you suggested to your Aunt Maxine that Magik 3 might just be available?" Ashley asked hopefully.

"Yup. For the low, low bargain price of thirty dollars," I said. "Ten bucks for each of us."

"Hank Zipzer, you are a total genius!"

Ashley shouted, slapping me a major high five. "What did your aunt say? Did she go for it?"

"Like guppies go for fish food," I said.

"*Zengawii!*" Frankie said, which is a magic word he made up when he was in Zimbabwe last summer. "Charlie the Clown is out and Magik 3 is in!"

We jumped up to do a victory dance, but before we could so much as wiggle our butts, Robert Upchurch appeared at our clubhouse door. Robert thinks he's our best friend just because he lives in our building. We keep trying to tell him he's not, but nothing we say will convince him of that. Even though he's only in third grade and we're all in fourth grade, he still sticks to us like peanut butter sticks to your braces.

"A word of advice," Robert chimed in without being asked. "Three-year-olds are a tough audience."

One annoying thing about Robert is that he offers information even when no one asks for it. Another annoying thing about Robert is that his information is almost always right. That's really hard to stomach.

"Guys, the little man does have a point," Frankie whispered to us. "Three-year-olds can barely pee in a toilet, how are they going to pick a card, any card, and remember what it is?"

"For ten bucks each, we'll make it work," said Ashley.

"We have something else we have to make work," I pointed out. "My aunt and uncle live all the way out on Long Island in Westhampton, and my parents are planning on spending the night. Do you think your parents will let you go?"

"Mine will," Robert said. "No problem here."

"Robert, the name of the group is Magik 3, not Magik 4," Ashley pointed out.

"That's three—Hank, Ashley, and me," Frankie added.

Robert looked at us with sad little puppy dog eyes on his sad little skinny face.

"Guys, you wouldn't go without me, would you?" he whined. "You're my best friends."

"No, we're not, Robert."

"What are you going to do? Leave me here all weekend?"

"Yes," we all said in unison.

"You can't go without me," Robert said. "Can you picture it? You out there on Long Island having ice cream and cake, and me, back here, eating a frozen breakfast burrito with freezer burn?"

Robert sure knows how to guilt you.

"You don't even have to pay me anything. I'll assist for free."

"Actually, you'd have to pay us," Ashley said.

"It's a deal," said Robert. "Seventy-five cents apiece."

"A dollar," said Ashley. I told you she's great with money matters.

"Give me a break, Ashley," said Robert. "I only get a third-grade allowance. And a dollar is seven-eighths of it."

Ashley glanced over at me to see what we should do. I couldn't decide. We would definitely have more fun if we left Robert behind in New York. But he really wanted to go, and we're not coldhearted kids. At least not totally.

CHAPTER 2

TEN EXCUSES WE COULD GIVE ROBERT FOR WHY HE CAN'T COME ON THE TRIP

1. Westhampton is at the beach, and it's very windy. Robert could get picked up by the wind and blown out to sea. Okay, it doesn't happen often, but it could.
2. A flock of seagulls could mistake Robert for a large rodent and swoop down and carry him off to their nest. Okay, it doesn't happen often, but it happens.
3. Robert is a walking, talking encyclopedia of facts. My Aunt Maxine gets a rash if she hears too many facts.
4. My Uncle Gary gets a rash if my Aunt Maxine gets a rash.

5. There is only a limited amount of oxygen in the car and let's face it, Robert just sucks in too much of it.
6. Robert is so skinny he could slip through a crack in the seat and we could lose him and never know it.
7. Robert has such bad allergies that the beach air would make his nose run so much there isn't enough Kleenex in all of Long Island to handle the slime.
8. The twins are having an ice-cream birthday cake and Robert himself has told me many times (way too many times) that ice cream gives him mucus build-up.
9. He'd have to sit next to my weird younger sister Emily in the backseat of the minivan and—

Wait a minute. Hank Zipzer, look what you just came up with. Robert would have to sit next to my sister Emily in the car! THAT MEANS I WOULDN'T HAVE TO SIT NEXT TO HER!!

Robert, my man. Good news! You're invited to a birthday party!

CHAPTER 3

WHEN I POINTED OUT to Frankie and Ashley that they wouldn't have to sit next to Emily either, they agreed to let Robert come along. No one wants to get stuck next to my younger sister for two hours in a backseat. It's not like she smells bad or anything. It's just that she talks all the time about weird stuff. The mating habits of iguanas is a favorite topic of hers.

"Okay, Robert, you can come," I said.

These words did not pop easily out of my mouth.

Robert jumped up and shook his bony butt in a victory dance, which is something I hope you never have to see.

"I told my aunt I'd let her know tomorrow if we can do the show," I said. "So check with your parents to see if Saturday and Sunday are okay."

"Wait, wait, wait . . ." Frankie said. "Zip, did you mean to say the party is *this* Saturday?"

"Yeah. Is there a problem?"

"Not a problem," said Frankie. "A tragedy. Make that a catastrophe."

"What's wrong?" I didn't like the look on Frankie's face.

"This Saturday is the Monster Movie Marathon on Channel 48," he said. "All monsters all the time. These twins are how old?"

"Three."

"That's bad. We all remember the three-year-old-birthday-party drill, right? Twelve thirty pizza. One o'clock magic show. One thirty piñata. Two o'clock cake and ice cream. Two thirty party favors. Two thirty-five balloon tied around kids' wrists. Two forty pick up. And parents, please be prompt."

"What are you, a walking invitation?" I said.

"Hear me, Zip." Frankie suddenly looked very serious. "That schedule puts the magic show smack in the middle of *The Mutant Moth That Ate Toledo* starring Vic Avalanche. I've been waiting to see that movie since the day I was born. Before, even."

"Frankie, are you saying you'd turn down a career opportunity for a stupid monster movie?" Ashley asked.

"I didn't hear that, Ashweena," Frankie said. "I can't believe that you, of all people, would call *The Mutant Moth That Ate Toledo* a stupid monster movie. It's an underground classic. Aboveground, too. I'm sorry, guys. I just can't go."

"Frankie," I said, sitting down on a cardboard box that was filled with our neighbor Mrs. Fink's extra bathrobes. "I just want you to know this. When I was on the phone with my Aunt Maxine, and she told the twins that we might come perform at their party, I heard them in the background. They weren't just yelling and screaming with excitement. They were crazed with happiness. They were jumping up and down on their pudgy little legs, and one of them, Zack I think, even threw himself on the hardwood floor. I heard the thud. But if you think a monster movie is more important than bringing that kind of joy into their little lives, then I think YOU should call them and tell them."

Frankie was chewing on his bottom lip, like he does when he's got a hard decision to make. I knew how much he loved monster movies. But I also knew how much I wanted Magik 3 to get this job. I have to admit, I can be pretty convincing when I want to be.

"But Zip," he said. "This is the original Mutant Moth movie. The one that started them all."

"I'm seeing the twins," I said. "I'm seeing their little smiling faces looking up at us on their special day. *You so good, you so good,* they yell."

"We could always tape the movie," Ashley said.

Of course. Where were my brains? I wish I had thought of that solution.

"Our VCR is busted," Frankie said, "and my dad doesn't want to fix it because he thinks we watch too much TV anyway."

"Okay then, here's the plan," I said, lowering my voice to almost a whisper. "We'll bring our own blank tape to my aunt's house. My

11

Uncle Gary has incredible video equipment and an awesome TV room. We'll tape the movie there and right after the party, we'll watch *The Mutant Moth That Ate Toledo* on his big-screen TV. No commercials, no interruptions, no parents hanging around. How great does that sound? Personally, I can't wait."

Frankie thought about it for a minute. "I need your solemn promise that we will tape the film and watch it right after the magic show, Zip. Nothing can come between me and that movie."

We put our hands one on top of another. Robert tried to sneak his hand in there, too. We let him. Like I said before, we're not totally coldhearted.

"A promise made is a promise kept," we all said at once.

"Okay, then I'll go," said Frankie.

"*Zengali!*" I hollered.

"Hank, don't even try," Frankie said, shaking his head. "The word is *zengawii*."

"Whatever," I said. "Here's to Magik 3 and our next paying performance!"

CHAPTER 4

THAT NIGHT, WE ALL checked with our parents.

Frankie's mom and dad said if he straightened up his room he could go.

Ashley's mom and dad said okay, too. They're both doctors and they had a conference they were supposed to go to and Ashley was going to stay with her grandmother anyway. I hope their conference was on how to give booster shots that don't hurt, because I think doctors could use a conference about that.

Robert checked with his mom, and unfortunately, she said she'd be thrilled to have him go with us. I don't blame her. If Robert were my son, and somebody said, "I'll take this walking encyclopedia off your hands for a day," boy, I'd jump at the chance.

Oddly enough, it was *my* parents who were the problem.

"I know you and Aunt Maxine discussed you performing at the party," my mom said, "but your schoolwork comes first."

"But Mom, I already told my friends it was a done deal."

"Let's go look at the chart and see if you can afford the time away this weekend."

I have a chart in my room that says what all my assignments are and when they're due. I didn't always have this chart. We just put it up a couple of weeks ago, when I found out I have learning challenges.

It's not like I'm stupid. It's just that certain things are really hard for me, like almost everything you learn in school. My dad had always thought I was lazy. The principal of my school, Leland Love, said I wasn't living up to my potential. My teacher, Ms. Adolf, said I wasn't focusing on my responsibilities. She also gave me four Ds on my report card. Wow, that really embarrassed me.

Then this nice woman who works at my school, Dr. Lynn Berger, gave me a bunch of tests that showed I'm not lazy or stupid—I just learn differently. One of the things she suggested is for me to have a chart in my room that reminds me of everything I have to do in school. That way, I don't forget my assignments and I focus better.

We went into my bedroom and looked at the chart. In the square for Monday, I had written the words SCIENCE PROJECT in red letters. Our actual science projects weren't due for three weeks, but by Monday, we had to pick our topic and say why we picked it. I didn't have a clue what I was going to do.

"Why don't you ask Emily for ideas?" my mother suggested. "She's excellent in science."

My sister Emily is nine annoying years old. Sometimes I think she's really an alien being. There's no other way to explain her behavior. Like she polishes her fingernails ten different colors. Twenty different colors if you count her toenails. And listen to this. She sleeps with her eyes open. I'm not kidding. She rolls her eyes back in her head and all you see is the white part.

"If I ask Emily, I already know what she'll

say," I answered. "She'll tell me to write about reptiles." Emily loves everything that's cold-blooded. If it's ugly and has scales, you can count her in.

"What's wrong with reptiles?" said a voice from behind me. It was none other than Lizard Girl herself, with Katherine, her pet iguana, wrapped around her neck like a scarf.

"Reptiles shed their own skin," I said. "How can you love something that walks right out of its own skin and leaves it there on the ground for other people to crunch on?"

"Hank, you are so narrow-minded," Emily said.

"At least I don't bite my toenails," I shot back.

"Stop it, you two," my mom said, holding up her hand, "or we're not going away for the weekend at all."

"Where are we going?" asked Emily.

"We're talking about going to Uncle Gary and Aunt Maxine's for the twins' birthday," my mom answered.

"We can't do that," Emily said. "What will we do with Katherine? You know she gets carsick."

One time, we took Katherine on a trip and she coughed up her lunch. She must have had grapes for dessert, because I'm sure I saw a whole green grape there on the backseat.

"Dad!" Emily screamed. "We need you in here right away. I'm calling a family meeting."

Family meetings in our house are not as good as they sound. My mom calls them to remind us not to leave our wet towels on the carpet after we take a shower. My dad calls them to yell at us when we have to pay late fees for rented videotapes. Emily calls them just to whine. I never call them. Why call for a meeting you don't want to attend in the first place?

My father walked into my bedroom, still holding the newspaper folded to the crossword puzzle. He's a crossword puzzle fanatic and proud of it.

"I'm in a very good mood," he said. "You're looking at the man who just solved today's crossword in six minutes and eleven seconds. A personal best."

"Congratulations, Dad," I said.

"Thank you, Hank. Now what's the problem, Emily? I'm in a problem-solving mood."

"Mom says we're making plans to go away for the weekend. No one has made plans for Katherine. Is she not a member of this family?"

"I vote no," I said immediately.

"She can't stay here alone," Emily whined. "She's afraid of the dark."

"Maybe Papa Pete can look after the beast," I suggested. Papa Pete is my grandpa and the single best human being in the whole world.

"Katherine is not a beast," Emily said.

"I was referring to you," I said.

"That's enough, Hank," my mom said. "Besides, Papa Pete can't look after Katherine. He's staying out in Westhampton for a couple of days. He wouldn't miss the twins' birthday. He's their grandfather, too."

"What did we do with the animals when we went to Niagara Falls last summer?" my dad asked.

"We left Cheerio with Mrs. Fink next door," I said. Cheerio is our beige dachshund dog. We call him that because he's always chasing his tail and when he spins around in a circle, he looks like a Cheerio. "I'll bet Mrs. Fink would watch him again. They really bonded."

"Katherine stayed at the pet store," Emily said. "George took care of her."

"You remember George, Dad," I said. "The pet store guy who looks like a gerbil."

"He does not," Emily said. "He just has a very furry beard."

"That starts at his eyebrows," I said.

"Emily, why don't you find the phone number of the pet store," Dad suggested.

"It's Pets for U and Me," Mom said. "The number is on the wall by the kitchen phone."

"Call and find out how much it would cost to keep Katherine there overnight," Dad suggested.

"Does this mean we're going?" I asked my mom. "I'll work on my science project in Westhampton, I promise."

My mom thought for a moment. "Okay, we'll go."

"Mom, you're the greatest," I said, giving her a big hug.

"It's about time you realized that," she said, hugging me back.

CHAPTER 5

THE TWINS' PARTY started at twelve thirty, so my dad told us we should be on the road Saturday morning by seven thirty, eight o'clock the latest. It's only about a three-hour drive to Westhampton, but he always builds in "lost time." That's the time when my dad is convinced it's a right turn and my mother says, "Stanley, please, just this once, turn left," and he doesn't, and we get totally lost.

My dad had rented a minivan for the trip and when he left to pick it up, he told us to be waiting outside the apartment building at eight o'clock sharp. I had called Frankie and Ashley and told them we were all meeting downstairs. Dad would drive by and get us, we'd drop off Katherine at Pets for U and Me, and then be on our way.

But when it was time to leave the apartment,

we couldn't find Katherine anywhere. She wasn't asleep in her cage. She wasn't in the bathtub where she likes to hang out. She wasn't under the dining room table sniffing for table scraps.

"This isn't like Katherine," Emily said. "She's never late."

"That's because she never *goes* anywhere," I pointed out.

My dad was not happy when he had to leave the minivan on the street for over an hour while we searched the apartment for Katherine. I couldn't believe that all four people in my family, plus Frankie and Ashley and Robert, were crawling around on our hands and knees looking for that scaly beast.

"Where could she be?" I said to my mom. "We've looked everywhere."

"You've got to think like an iguana," Emily said. "Put yourself in Katherine's shoes."

"Okay," I said. "I feel myself in four little tiny baby Nikes, size one, extra wide. Ouch, they're hurting my claws!"

Frankie and Ashley cracked up.

"Hey guys, I found her!" called Robert from the other side of the room.

He was crouched over the potted palm tree next to our front door. Sure enough, there was Katherine, her nasty little face poking out from behind one of the palm leaves.

"Katherine!" cried Emily. "Come to mama!" She reached into the tree to pick her up, and Katherine hissed at her like she was a rattlesnake with gas. Lots of gas.

"What's the matter, sweetie pie?" Emily said in her baby reptile voice.

"I'm sure she's stressed," Robert said. "She's had a very terrifying experience."

Emily looked at Robert and—grab your stomachs because this is disgusting—she got all gooey eyed.

"What a nice thing to say, Robert," she said, still in her baby reptile voice. "I didn't know you cared so much about iguana moods."

"Actually," said Robert, "I'm fond of the whole reptile kingdom, including the bullfrog, the Gila monster, and the gecko, my favorite."

Could you just barf?

Thank goodness my dad got down to business and cut this icky conversation short.

"Emily, get a box for Katherine. Let's hurry,

everyone. We're going to be late for the party."

We gathered Katherine and all our stuff and piled into the elevator. The minivan was parked outside, and luckily for us, we didn't even get a parking ticket, since my father had double-parked. As soon as she saw the car, Emily yelled out, "Shotgun!"

"Not in this lifetime," I said. I turned to my mother, who was loading our stuff in the back. "Mom, tell her she's not old enough. Plus, we have guests."

"Absolutely, and I'm one of them," said Robert. "So I call shot—"

I didn't even let him finish the word.

"Forget it, Robert. We had a deal, remember? You're next to Lizard Girl. Way in the back."

It took some wrestling, but I got Emily to move into the backseat by the window on the driver's side. Robert climbed in next to her. That still left one seat in the back, next to the two geekoids.

"I can't sit there," Ashley said. "I get carsick."

"I do, too," I said.

"No, you don't," my mom called out from the back.

"Well, I would if I had to sit next to *them*," I said.

Frankie took a deep breath.

"Okay," he said, "I'm going in. If I don't survive the trip, give my signed Yankees baseball to my brother."

That's what you call true friendship. Frankie and I get along almost all the time because we'll do anything for each other. The only thing we ever fight about is that Frankie is a Yankees fan and I love, I mean *love*, the Mets. We've been able to stay best friends in spite of that.

Frankie climbed in the backseat next to Robert and wedged himself as close as he could to the window. One inch further and he would've been sitting outside the car on the curb. He drew a line with his fingernail along the upholstery.

"Robert," he said. "If you cross this line, there will be consequences. Large ones and small ones."

"Can you give me an example, please?" asked Robert. Frankie reached over and gave

Robert a noogie on his head, not too hard, just enough to make his point. Robert squealed like a kitten.

"And that's a small consequence," Frankie said.

Ashley and I slid into the middle bench. And my mom, without even calling it, got shotgun. I tell you, adults have it made.

We drove down 78th Street, which is our block, past Mr. Kim's grocery store. He was outside, using his green garden hose to put fresh water in the buckets of roses. We passed our school, P.S. 87. It was closed up tight, which is the way I like it best.

When we reached Columbus Avenue, we stopped at the pet store and dropped Katherine off. George was waiting outside, and he was so happy to see her. Mr. Furry and Miss Scaly.

We drove through Central Park. Lots of people were out walking their dogs. I saw a dachshund that looked just like Cheerio, except he was dressed in a plaid overcoat with four little red boots. Once on Halloween, we put a sailor hat on Cheerio. He didn't like that and started doing his spinning thing. That time, he spun around so fast that the sailor hat flew off his head and landed directly on top of my dad's head. It was amazing. If I knew the number, I would've called Ripley's Believe It or Not. From that day on, we realized that Cheerio was a dog who will not wear people clothes. I give him credit for that.

As we headed to the Triborough Bridge that takes you out of town, I turned and looked back at the skyline of Manhattan. Whenever I look at all the skyscrapers poking their tops up into the clouds, I always feel proud that New York is my city and lucky that I get to live in such an exciting place.

We settled in for the ride to Westhampton. My mom, who is working on inventing healthy snack foods for the twenty-first century, offered everyone a taste of her new salt-free, wheat-free, taste-free soy pretzel snack that she stuffed with rice cheese. We all said we were really full.

When the city was no longer in view, my mom turned in her seat and said the dreaded words.

"Let's sing some travel songs."

She does this on every car trip we take. She

has a list in her head of really horrible songs—ones that are *both* long and bad—like "Found a Peanut", "My Darling Clementine", and of course, the always awful "Row Row Row Your Boat."

"That sounds like fun," said Robert, and Emily agreed.

What is wrong with them? Don't they know the difference between fun and not-fun?

"No singing," I begged. The last thing I wanted to hear was Robert belting out "Row Row Row Your Boat" in his nasal little twang.

"Then how about a game?" my mom suggested.

"Great idea," said Robert. "Why don't we drill each other on multiplication tables?"

"Why don't I drill you through the back-seat," whispered Frankie.

"I've got it," Emily said. "Let's shout out Amazing Iguana Facts."

Can you believe this girl and I come from the same mother and father?

"Iguanas are born with eighty teeth, but by the time they get to be Mr. Zipzer's age, they have one hundred and twenty teeth," Robert said, without missing a beat.

"Robert," Emily said, "that is fascinating."

I turned around and stared at Emily. I have shared a house with this girl since the day she was born, but I had never heard that tone of voice come out of her. It sounded so sweet, like maple syrup covering a buckwheat pancake.

"Furthermore," Robert went on, staring straight at Emily, "did you know that two-thirds of an iguana's length is its tail?"

Emily cracked up.

"Yes!" She giggled. "And when attacked, the iguana can break off its own tail."

"After which, it actually grows a new tail," added Robert.

Robert and Emily gave each other a high five. They were in nerd heaven. I glanced at Ashley and Frankie, and their eyes were rolling into the back of their heads.

"Can we turn on the radio now?" I begged my mom. "I don't even care if it's your oldies station." Anything to cover up the iguana fest that was oozing out of the backseat.

It was after twelve thirty when we finally reached Westhampton. We drove through some woods into a pretty little town. Past the town was a clump of houses all painted pink and blue and yellow. They were new and low to the ground, not like the skyscrapers in Manhattan. Even though they were a few blocks away from the ocean, you could still see the sand underneath the lawns and in between the houses and on the sides of the streets. I recognized my Uncle Gary and Aunt Maxine's house because my aunt had tied a bunch of "Happy Birthday" balloons around the shiny copper mailbox.

We pulled into the driveway. Zack and Jake came running out to greet us, wearing red boots and capes.

"They're here, they're here," they shouted. And when I say shouted, I mean *shouted*. Those little guys had some powerful lungs.

"Ank," they said, jumping on me and spraying spit into my face. "Ank, did you bring us a present?"

Papa Pete came running out to say hello. Even though he's going to be sixty-eight next June 26, he's in really good shape. With his bushy mustache and strong, hairy arms, he looked like a grizzly bear in a red sweatsuit.

"How are all my grandkids?" Papa Pete said. Ashley and Frankie and Robert aren't really related to him, but Papa Pete likes to call us all his grandkids anyway. He gave me a big pinch on the cheek.

"I love this cheek and everything that's attached to it," he said. He pinched Ashley and Frankie, too, but when he went for Robert's cheek, his fingers just slid right off.

"I've got to introduce you to pastrami sandwiches," he said to Robert. "Put a little meat on those bones."

For his whole life, Papa Pete ran The Crunchy Pickle, the deli that my mom took over. Like I told you, my mom is trying to change it into a healthy deli that serves soy salami and vegetarian bologna and other taste-free treats. But when Papa Pete was making the sandwiches, people said they were the best in town.

"Who are you?" Zack said to Frankie, pointing a chocolate-covered finger right up at Frankie's face.

"I'm Frankie, little dude. Nice to meet you."

"What's so nice about it?" Zack said.

Ashley stepped up to help.

"Nice to meet you is something you say when you meet a new friend," she explained to Zack. "It's good manners."

"I don't have good manners," Zack said.

"Me, either," Jake said.

That was pretty obvious, so I thought maybe I should change the subject.

"Hey, are you guys ready for a great magic show?" I said, giving them my best smile, the one where I show my top and bottom teeth.

"I hate magic," cried Jake.

"Yeah, me, too," screamed Zack.

"It stinks," said Jake.

"Yeah, stinks," added Zack.

Zack gave me a swift kick in the leg. Jake bit me on the hand.

That was my first clue that it was going to be a very long afternoon.

CHAPTER 6

MY AUNT MAXINE came running outside and threw her arms around my mom. She's my mother's younger sister. They both have curly blond hair that flies off in all directions, but at that moment, Aunt Maxine looked like she had stuck her finger in an electric socket. Her hair was standing straight up and her eyes were popping out of her head.

"I thought you'd never get here," she said, giving me a kiss on the head.

"I'm sorry we're so late, Max," my mom said. "We had reptile problems."

"Who doesn't?" my aunt said. I don't think she even heard what my Mom said, otherwise she would have said something like, "*What happened? Did spotted frogs invade your dining room?*" You don't just ignore it when someone says they have reptile problems.

"Aunt Maxine, I'd like to introduce you to Magik 3," I said, pointing to Ashley and Frankie. "Plus one," I added, when Robert stuck his face in front of her. "There's no extra charge for him."

"Come inside quickly," Aunt Maxine said. "We need entertainment! The kids are going crazy."

"How many are in there?" Frankie asked nervously.

"Seventeen, but it feels like a hundred and nine," Aunt Maxine answered. "They got into the M & M's—the entire jumbo bag—and they're pretty sugared up."

"Maybe we should raise our fee," Ashley whispered.

"It's my family," I whispered back. "We can't ask for more."

We weren't even inside the front door when we were pelted with M & M's. Most of the kids were hiding behind the couches and chairs. Their parents were in the backyard, sipping coffee and trying to ignore the candy-chucking that was going on inside. A blue M & M hit me in the forehead.

"Hey, you could put an eye out doing that!" I said. I couldn't believe my own voice. That was something my mom said all the time, and here I was, saying those very same words. I was turning into my mom!

"Kids! Kids!" Papa Pete called out. "Candy goes *in* your face, not *on* it."

"Cousin Hank and his friends have come all the way here to put on a magic show for you," said Aunt Maxine. "Won't that be fun?"

The answer came in a hailstorm of M & M's.

Papa Pete whispered to us, "I think you better start the show right away. The audience is restless."

"Okay," I said.

"Not so fast, Zip," said Frankie, grabbing my arm. "You better find the VCR first."

"I will," I said. "Don't worry about it."

Frankie looked at his watch.

"*The Mutant Moth That Ate Toledo* starts in ten minutes," he said. "We have to set up the tape before we begin the show."

Ashley could hear the nervous tone in Frankie's voice.

"I'll tell you what," she said. "Frankie and I

will set up for the show, and Hank, you find the VCR. Okay, Hank?"

"No problem," I said. I could see Frankie relax. Ashley Wong is a great stress buster.

"Aunt Maxine, where's Uncle Gary?" I asked.

"He's right there," she said. I turned to a corner of the room, and saw a guy in floppy shoes and a clown wig trying to make balloon animals. His clown lipstick was smeared all over his face. His red clown nose, which was attached by a rubber band, was sitting on his forehead so he could blow into the balloons. He was blowing and blowing until the veins in his neck stuck out, but the balloon would not inflate.

"Hey Uncle Gary," I said. "Is it all right if I use your VCR?"

"It's in the den," he said. He didn't sound happy.

I ran out to the car and got the blank tape we had brought. When I came back in, the kids were smushing chocolate chip cookies into one another's faces. Frankie was setting up his magic table in the living room. Ashley was putting up the Magik 3 sign. Robert, who was supposed to be helping, was following Emily around like a pathetic puppy.

I went into the den, closed the door, and looked around for the television. What I saw looked like an electronics department store. There were five remote controls on the coffee table. Each one was a different length and had different buttons in different places. On the wall, there was one big television and three little ones running down the side of it. But that's just the beginning. There was also a CD player, a DVD player, a CD that recorded the DVD, a PlayStation One, a PlayStation Two, and an empty space next to that—I guess that was just waiting for a PlayStation Three.

I looked at all the equipment, and if you had offered me a zillion dollars, I couldn't have told you which machine I should put the tape in. The entire cabinet was filled with lights. Red ones, green ones, white ones. Blinking ones, flashing ones, steady ones. Digital numbers changing constantly on dials that looked like the instrument panel of a fighter jet. I stared at all the lights and numbers. They were like a magnet for my eyes. I couldn't stop looking at them, but I couldn't really see them, either. They were just a big blur.

Come on, Hank. Focus. You can't just stand here and look at the pretty lights. Frankie is counting on you. You promised.

I jumped up and down on one foot, trying to shake my brain into action. The numbers and lights were all there like they were laughing at me, daring me to read them.

I know what to do.

I squinched up my face and closed my eyes really tight, then opened them up really wide.

There! That would do it. Everything would be crystal-clear now.

I wish.

When I opened my eyes, everything looked just like it did before. I walked up to the machines and started poking them, to find the one that had a flap that would open for the tape to slide in. I got it on the third machine.

Good deal. This wasn't going to be so hard. I was in business.

As I slid the tape in, the machine ate it like I eat a cheeseburger. Now I just had to turn on the TV and tape the movie. Easy. No problem.

Uh-oh. Major problem.

I flicked on the television and went to Channel 48, but it wasn't the same channel 48 that we get at home. In fact, none of the channels were the same as ours. I surfed around and didn't even recognize half the shows that were on. My aunt and uncle must have 500 channels.

I opened the door and stepped out into the hall. I thought that if I could find Frankie, he'd help me figure out the channel where the movie was playing. Frankie wasn't in the hall, but one of the three-year-old boys was.

"I want to see a dinosaur on TV," he said, trying to push his way into the den.

"I just talked to Mr. Dinosaur," I said, "and he told me that all the dinosaurs are napping right now so you have to come back later when they wake up."

"But—"

"Bye-bye. So long. Ta-ta for now. Later, dude," I said as I slipped back inside the door and waited until I heard his footsteps fade away down the hall.

What now? Breathe. Breathe fast. The clock is ticking.

I picked up another remote and studied the front of it. There was a button that said "information." That's what I needed—information. Such as what channel the movie was on.

I pushed the button. Great news! The screen showed a program guide that listed all the programs and what channel they were on. Bad news! The information was rolling by at a pace only a speed reader could follow.

I tried to read the words, and I caught some of them. *Tennis. Cooking with*— It went by too fast. And there it was—*The Mutant Moth That Ate Toledo.*

It came on at the bottom. Next to it was a description of the movie, and by the time I got to the column with what channel it was on, it was gone—disappeared into the top of the screen.

"Hank, get out here," Ashley called from down the hall. "Your aunt says we have to start the show RIGHT NOW!"

What channel was it? Thirty-six. Right. I'm sure that was the channel number I saw.

I got the remote and programmed in thirty-six. I pushed the RECORD NOW button. The red record light came on, and I felt a great sense of victory.

I was the king of these machines. They had tried to get me, but in the end, they couldn't touch me. I am the machine master.

The door flew open and Jake came running in. Or maybe it was Zack. I couldn't tell them apart.

"Why are you in here?" he hollered. "I'm going to tell my daddy."

"Your daddy already knows," I said. "Come on, let's go do some magic."

"I hate magic."

"Yeah, I know." I said. "Come on, I'll race you."

He kicked me and ran out of the room.

Oh right, now I knew. It was Zack.

Jake bites. Zack kicks. I've got to remember that.

CHAPTER 7

WHEN I WALKED into the living room, my mom and Aunt Maxine were trying to herd the kids onto the living room rug. It wasn't easy. As soon as they got one kid sitting down, another one popped up like a jack-in-the-box.

"Sit down, Jackson," Aunt Maxine said to a cute little guy with a buzzed haircut. "Don't you want to see the magic show?"

"I don't want to sit next to him," Jackson said, pointing to a kid named Benjamin. "His diapers stink."

"I'm not wearing diapers," Benjamin cried. "I'm wearing pull-ups."

"They still stink," said Jackson.

"That hurts Benjamin's feelings," my mom said. "Do you want to do that, Jackson?"

"Yes," said Jackson.

"I don't think you really mean that, Jackson."

"Yes, I do. His smell hurts my nose."

"Emily, can you help us out here?" my mom asked. Emily and Robert were in the corner of the room, trying to name each tropical fish in the fish tank.

"Mom, I can't right now. We're watching the catfish suck algae off the glass."

"Go help your mom," Robert said. "I'll call you when he starts sucking on the filter."

Emily went up to a bunch of girls and said, "Come with me and sit down."

The girls just stood there, holding hands and staring at her fingernails, which, as I said, are all painted a different color.

"You have weird fingers," one of the girls said.

"Mom!" screamed Emily. "They're not listening."

"Step aside, Emily," I said. "Let a pro show you how it's done."

"Like they'll listen to you," she snapped.

"Come on, girls. Let's all pretend we're bunnies and hop over to the magic show," I suggested.

I put my hands on my head like two floppy

bunny ears and started to hop. I turned around, and, holy cow, there they were—a bunch of baby bunnies hopping behind me. We all hopped over to the rug. And I was hoping, as I hopped, that no one was watching.

"Now let's all jump into our bunny holes." I squatted on the rug, and they did exactly the same thing, sitting down like little angels. I looked over at Emily.

"Hey, some of us hop it, some of us don't," I said.

I looked over at Aunt Maxine and she mouthed the words, "Thank you." I felt good.

Frankie had set up his magic table in front of the stone fireplace. I took my place on one side of him, and Ashley stood on the other. Frankie had put on his cape and top hat. Ashley had put our name, Magik 3, in rhinestones across the front of his top hat. She loves to decorate everything with rhinestones.

"Boys and girls," Ashley began. "Welcome to our show."

"We're not girls," the girls giggled. "We're bunnies. Let's hop!"

Ashley put her finger to her lips and tried to

shhhhh them. But they were into their bunny thing, and went on hopping. Ashley looked over at Frankie and shrugged.

"Poof," he said, waving his magic wand. "Now you're girls again."

"Poof," they said. "Now we're poofy heads."

"Frankie," Papa Pete whispered from the sidelines. "Get on with the show. Quickly."

"For my first trick," Frankie began, "I'll need a volunteer."

Seventeen pairs of eyes stared back at him blankly. No one moved.

"Maybe the birthday boys would want to help," Papa Pete said.

Ashley picked one of the twins. It was either Jake or Zack. I couldn't tell which one until he either bit or kicked. He came forward.

"Did you clean your ears today?" Frankie asked him. Then he mouthed to me, "Which one is it?" I shrugged. I really had no idea.

My cousin didn't answer, he just gave Frankie a swift kick in the shin.

"Zack," I said to Frankie. "It's definitely Zack."

"Well, Zack," Frankie said, "I think maybe you didn't clean your ears, because look what I found inside them." Frankie held a metal cup next to Zack's ear, and made it look like quarters were falling into the cup. It's a great trick, unless you happen to be my cousin Zack. He started to scream his powerful little lungs out.

"I don't want money growing inside my head!" he shrieked, running to his mother.

"It's okay, honey," Aunt Maxine said. "It's just magic."

"I don't want magic in my head!" he said. "I want to ride on a fire truck."

I understood. Fire trucks are cool. I always wanted to be the guy who rides at the back of the hook and ladder, way up high at the steering wheel. That has to be the best job in the whole world, except maybe being the owner of Disney World.

Aunt Maxine carried Zack out to the backyard. This was a good thing. Now we'd know which twin was left, without having to wait to get kicked.

"How about a card trick?" Ashley suggested. "No one could possibly be scared by a card."

"Good idea," Frankie said.

By now, drops of sweat were rolling down his face and pooling up in his dimple. Frankie's dimple makes him look so handsome—all the girls in our grade love it. But now his dimple was really coming in handy, to catch all the sweat.

Frankie picked up a deck of cards. He fanned out the cards in his hand, and told Jake to "pick a card any card." Jake reached out and grabbed about twenty cards. Ashley took most of the cards and put them back in the deck, leaving Jake with just the nine of diamonds.

"Look at the card," Frankie said to Jake. Jake started to turn the card around. "No, no, don't show it to me," Frankie said.

"Why?" asked Jake.

"Because if you don't tell me, I will guess it. And when I guess it, that's the magic part."

"But I *want* to tell you," Jake said, starting to get really red in the face.

"Let's see if Frankie the Magician can guess the card," Ashley said.

She took Jake's hand and helped him push the card back in the deck. Frankie shuffled the deck with lots of fanfare, then waved his hand over the deck and said, "*Zengawii!*"

He held up the deck so everyone could see the bottom card. It was the nine of diamonds. Papa Pete applauded. He was the only one.

"Jake, tell us all, is your card the nine of diamonds?" Frankie asked.

Jake stared for a moment at Frankie, then at Ashley.

Frankie asked again, "Is this your card?"

Jake opened his mouth. He was going to answer. All eyes were on him. He knew it, too. He stood as tall as he could without falling over.

"What's a nine look like?" he asked. All the adults in the room laughed and Jake burst out crying. This wasn't exactly the big ending we had been hoping for.

"Does anyone here know what a nine looks like?" Frankie said, his voice cracking.

The only one in the whole room who raised his hand was Robert.

CHAPTER 8

WHEN THE MONSTER TWINS from Mars finally fell asleep, it was truly something to celebrate.

It happened somewhere after the fried chicken dinner but before the second birthday cake. First one of them passed out, his cheek landing with a little plop in the frosting. That was Jake. I know that because he only eats frosting and Zack only eats cake. Right after that, Zack fell asleep sitting straight up, mid-chew, with his fork still in his hand. We knew he was asleep because he had stopped kicking.

Ashley, Frankie, and I cheered—but very quietly. We were taking no chances on waking them up.

Papa Pete picked up Jake and Uncle Gary took Zack and carried them off to their room.

"How about I set you kids up in the den," Aunt Maxine said.

"Excellent idea," Frankie said. "A few sleeping bags, a big-screen TV, and the best scary movie ever made."

"What movie is that?" asked Aunt Maxine.

"*The Mutant Moth That Ate Toledo*," Frankie answered. "I've been waiting ten years, three months, and fourteen days to see it. And tonight's the night, thanks to my man Hank who recorded it for us this afternoon."

"That was nice of you, Hank." My mom smiled.

"What are best friends for?" I said.

"Two of you can sleep on the couch," Aunt Maxine said. "There's a blow-up mattress in the closet along with the futon."

"That's only enough beds for four," Robert said. "Someone's going to have to sleep on the floor."

"We hope you're comfortable, Robert," we all said.

"Hey, that's not fair," Emily piped up.

"Fine," I said, "Let's be fair and take a vote. Everyone who thinks Robert should sleep on the floor raise your hand." Ashley, Frankie, and I raised our hands.

"All opposed?" I asked. Robert and Emily raised their hands.

"Three to two," I said. "Majority rules. Robert sleeps on the floor."

I love democracy.

We set our stuff up in the den, and made it into the most comfortable place you've ever been in. Frankie and I took the couch. Ashley had the blow-up mattress. Emily had the futon. And just to show we weren't totally heartless, we used the throw pillows from the couch to make Robert a soft spot on the carpet to rest his bony little head.

"Thanks, guys," Robert said. He flopped down on his new bed, but the pillows separated and made a deep crevasse that he almost disappeared into.

"Look," said Ashley, "*The Pillows That Ate Robert*. We have our own horror movie right here before the main feature."

"Help, get me out of here," Robert squeaked from under the pillows that were stacked two deep.

It's not easy rescuing a kid from under a huge stack of pillows when you're laughing so hard you think you're going to throw up.

"Hey, let's start the movie," Frankie said, getting serious all of a sudden. "And everybody quiet. I don't want to miss the opening. That's when the moth slimes out of his cocoon."

"Don't worry, Frankie," Ashley said. "It's taped. We can watch it as many times as we want."

There was a knock on the door and my mom came in carrying a tray of snacks.

"Look what I brought," she said. "Celery sticks stuffed with tofu cream cheese and pimiento."

If you've never tried it, this is a combo to stay as far away from as possible.

"Thanks, Mom," I said, closing the door behind her. "Sounds yummy."

"Where's the tape?" Frankie said. "I'll load it up."

"No need to do that," I told him. "It's in the machine. Rewound and ready to go. All we have to do is press PLAY."

I walked up to the bank of machines and turned on the TV.

"Wow," said Frankie, "that's one humungous

television screen. This is going to be so cool. I've got to say this, Zip. Coming here was a brilliant idea. This is going to be so much better than watching *The Mutant Moth That Ate Toledo* on our little TV at home."

He held up his hand for a high five as I passed him.

There was another knock on the door and Papa Pete stuck his head in.

"Is your mother anywhere in the vicinity?" he whispered. "I see she's already been here," he added, looking at the tray of stuffed celery with pimientos.

He came into the room, carrying a big bowl filled with ice cream bars. Not just ice cream sandwiches, either. But popsicles with root beer on one side and cherry on the other. There were also Fudgsicles, Eskimo Pies, and strawberry bonbons.

Some grandparents might bring you an ice cream sandwich for a treat, or maybe a Fudgsicle. But how many grandfathers would bring you an *assortment* of ice cream bars? Mine would, and did. I am so lucky.

Papa Pete took the celery tray away. "I'll

dispose of this," he said, and then left.

I cleared my throat and stood right next to the television.

"Ladies and gentlemen, welcome to the Zipzer Theatre. We are proud to be showing *The Mutant Moth That Burped Up Toledo.*"

"Come on, Zip. Just push the button already," Frankie yelled from his place on the couch.

And I did! I pushed PLAY and hurled myself across the room to take my place on the couch just as the movie started.

The tape crackled with static and then the picture came on. A woman's face filled the screen. She was wearing a pearl necklace and was holding up her wrist to show us a matching bracelet. She reminded us that there were only nineteen of these sets left, and we better call in a hurry. The phone number flashed on and off at the bottom of the screen.

"What is this? *The Moth That Ate the Home Shopping Network?*" Emily said.

"Come on, Zip. Stop messing with me and start the movie," Frankie said.

"Someone probably switched the tape," I

said, "but the Zip Master has everything under control." Boy, was I hoping that was true.

I went to the machine and ejected the tape. *Uh-oh.* It was my tape, the one I had written MOTH on with a green marker so it would stand out against the white label. I stuck it back in and looked for the FAST FORWARD button. I pushed it and the tape sped quickly ahead. I waited for about thirty seconds and pushed PLAY again.

Oh, no! There she was again, the woman holding up that stupid bracelet, but now there were only fifteen left.

"What's going on, Hank?" Frankie sounded like he was starting to get nervous. As a matter of fact, so was I. *Where was the movie?*

"Give me a minute to figure this out," I said. "It's got to be on here somewhere." I pushed fast forward again. I could feel my heart beating.

"He's such a moron, he probably taped the wrong thing," Emily said.

"Not now, Emily, I don't need that now," I barked.

I pushed PLAY again and prayed that the

bracelet lady would disappear. And she did.

Thank goodness!

Only now, in her place, was a guy in tights, pulling himself up and down on an exercise machine. The Ab Flab, I think it was. There were plenty of those left for sale.

"Hank, what's going on?" said Frankie. I had never heard him speak in that tone of voice before.

"I'm sure I taped it right," I said.

"Did you check the time and channel in the guide?" Robert said, picking up the book that lists all the programs for the month.

"I can't use that book," I said. "There's too many little letters and numbers and columns. I get confused. I used the guide on the screen."

"Well, what did it say?" said Ashley. "Did you see the time and channel?"

I felt like I was being attacked from all sides. Frankie flew off the couch and grabbed the guide from Robert's hands. He flipped the pages furiously until he got to the right one.

"Here it is. *The Mutant Moth that Ate Toledo*. One P.M. to three P.M. Channel 336. Tell me that's what you taped," he said to me, pointing to the listing in the program guide.

"What channel was that?" I asked.

"Three, three, six," he barked back, pronouncing each number very clearly.

My heart sank. I remembered now. I had set the recorder to Channel 36. I must not have seen that first number. It went by so fast, my eyes couldn't focus.

I froze. I didn't know what to do or what to say. All Frankie wanted was to see this one movie. I promised him that I would take care of it. We shook hands on it. I swore I would do it.

And now, I had messed up. I had totally and completely messed up, just because I couldn't read the numbers moving so fast on the screen.

My stupid brain, I thought. I hate it. Honestly and truly, I hate every cell of it.

CHAPTER 9

I'VE KNOWN FRANKIE TOWNSEND since before we were born. Our moms always tell stories about how they used to walk in the park together when they were pregnant with us.

We've been through lots of tough times together. When Frankie fell off the jungle gym in preschool, he didn't want to cry in front of everyone. I stood in front of him so the other kids couldn't see him cry. When I peed in my pants in kindergarten just before the Thanksgiving pageant, Frankie gave me the extra pair of pants he kept in his cubby. And he never told anyone about my accident.

We've had a few fights, like the time we were camping and I ate the whole 3 Musketeers bar and didn't save him a bite. I tried to tell him I saved him the wrapping because it was made out of real silver, but he didn't go for it. Still, in all our ten years together, I had never seen Frankie Townsend as mad as he was that night.

I tried to explain what happened, how the numbers on the television were going too fast for me. In the middle of my explanation, he picked up his sleeping bag and stormed out of the room.

"Where are you going?" Ashley asked him.

"I'd rather sleep with the twins than stay in here with him," he said.

If I didn't know before how mad he was, that clinched it. Our friendship was over. I started to pace around the room.

"He's never going to talk to me again," I said to Ashley. "Every time he sees me from now on, he's going to ignore me." I stopped pacing. "What happens if we're in the elevator together? We're just going to stand there in total silence looking at the floor numbers change."

"Hank," Ashley said, "would you like me to try to talk to Frankie?"

"It won't do any good, Ash. I've just lost my best friend."

"I'll be your best friend," Robert volunteered. Why was that not helping? "Hey, want to get a slice and a Coke after school on Monday?" the clueless one went on.

"Robert, do I have to draw you a map?" I said. "I can't have this conversation right now, and besides, you're not best friend material."

"I think he is," Emily said.

"Fine," I said. "Then you and Robert can be best friends. Have fun counting iguana scales. And think of me, because my life as I know it is over."

"Hank," Ashley said. "Frankie is just mad. He really, really, really wanted to see that movie."

"Rub it in," I said. "Don't you think I know that?"

"Give him some time to get over it," Ashley said. "He'll cool down, you'll say you're sorry, he'll say, 'Hey, that's okay, Zip,' and everything will be back the way it was."

What Ashley didn't understand was that to me, this was about more than taping a movie for Frankie. This was Frankie realizing that he couldn't trust me. Why would anyone want a best friend he couldn't trust? I always knew this was going to happen—that one day, Frankie would finally see I wasn't a friend worth having. He's so smart, he can do everything. And what can I do?

I mean, what can I do?

My brain was going a mile a minute, and I must've said something like, "What can I do?" out loud, because when I looked up, Emily was answering me.

"You can ask me to help you next time," she said. Could this be? My *sister* was offering first aid to *me*. "Really, Hank, if there's something you can't do and I can, why not ask for help?"

This was Emily Grace Zipzer talking.

"Easy for you to say," I answered her. "Do you know how hard it is to live with Miss Perfect? It's embarrassing for me to admit that *I* need help from *you* when you're seventeen months younger than me. I would look like a complete idiot."

"I'm not perfect, Hank," Emily said. She actually sounded nice.

"I think you are," Robert piped up. I think he surprised himself, because as soon as he said it, his ears turned bright red, like he was wearing two beets attached to his head.

"Robert, do you really think so?" Emily said. She was doing that maple syrup thing with her voice again.

"I'm going to find Frankie," I said.

"I'll come with you," said Ashley.

"Listen, Ash, I think I need to talk to Frankie myself."

Ashley nodded. I knew she'd understand, even if it meant she had to stay alone in the den with Mr. Nerd and Miss Nerdess. She's the kind of person who'll do a thing like that for a friend.

I went upstairs looking for Frankie.

He wasn't in any of the upstairs rooms, so I went back downstairs. Finally, I found him in his sleeping bag under the dining room table.

"What are you doing here?" I asked.

"I couldn't sleep," Frankie said. "What do you want?"

"I want to say I'm sorry," I told him.

"Sorry doesn't help," he said.

I didn't answer.

"It was so easy, Hank," he said. There was a lot of frustration in his voice. "I waited so long and it was so easy. All you had to do was punch in three numbers and push the record button. Anybody can do that."

"I can't," I said. "Just because it's easy for you, doesn't mean it's easy for me."

"Can we not talk about this now?" Frankie said.

"When can we talk about it?" I asked.

"I don't know. Later. Sometime. Whenever."

"When?"

"When we get back to the city. All right? Good night."

I wanted to go on, but Frankie pulled his sleeping bag up over his head in a way that left no doubt that he was done talking.

"Good night, Frankie," I said.

He didn't answer.

CHAPTER 10

I TRIED TO GO TO SLEEP, but I couldn't. So I made a list.

EIGHT THINGS THAT ARE HARD FOR ME AND EASY FOR FRANKIE

1. Spelling, especially hard words like what you call the person who lives next door to you. You know, your next-door *naybor* or is it *neibor* or *neyber*? I don't know, so don't ask me. *(Frankie is a dictionary with a mouth.)*
2. Remembering words to songs. *(Frankie is a human karaoke machine.)*
3. Learning how to play an instrument, except for the tambourine and who wants to play that? *(Frankie plays the sax and knows over ten songs by heart.)*

4. Finding my backpack. *(Frankie's backpack is where it belongs, on his back.)*
5. Remembering phone numbers. *(Frankie not only remembers phone numbers, he remembers area codes, too.)*
6. Reading a map. *(Frankie is a human compass.)*
7. Writing a letter. *(Frankie is the King of Thank-You Notes.)*
8. Reading the program guide on the television screen. Obviously, I am a total flop at that.

CHAPTER 11

WE GOT UP EARLY the next morning, had some breakfast, and then loaded into the minivan for the ride back to the city.

Let me tell you about the ride home. First, I want you to stop reading and just listen. Do you hear anything? Well, neither did I. Our car on the ride home was about as quiet as a metal box covered in cement and buried way under the ocean floor halfway to China.

What I'm trying to say is that Frankie didn't say one word to me. Zilch. Zip. Nada.

He gave me the Big Freeze, and boy, was I cold.

CHAPTER 12

AFTER WE GOT HOME, Frankie went up to his apartment without saying so much as "I'll meet you later in the clubhouse." I'm sure Ashley was feeling caught in the middle of our fight, because she tried to be cheerful and make us laugh. It didn't work, though. You couldn't have made Frankie Townsend laugh if you had tickled him under the arms with a twenty-foot feather. Ashley even offered to bring blueberry muffins for our walk to school the next morning, but Frankie just shrugged and said, "Thanks, Ash, but I don't think I'll be hungry."

Robert asked if he could go with Emily and my father to pick up Katherine from the pet store. He said he was looking forward to a chance to spend some quality time with our iguana. What kind of kid wants to spend time with an iguana? If you think about it, what kind of kid wants to spend time with my sister?

I was pretty stressed from all that happened, and was hoping I could just kick back and lie on the couch, which is one of my favorite things to do. So after I picked up Cheerio from Mrs. Fink's apartment, I flopped down on the couch and put him on my stomach for a big belly scratch. That is one of his favorite things to do. It's so cute the way he looks up at you and yips like a little puppy. His other favorite thing is licking the bricks on the fireplace. Don't ask me why he does that; I told you he was slightly nuts.

I hadn't even been flopped on the couch for two minutes when my mom unflopped me.

"Up and at 'em," she said, holding out her hand to pull me up.

"Mom, I just got comfortable."

"Well, you can be comfortable later, because there's a little thing called your science project waiting for you. Your topic is due tomorrow, and you promised . . ."

"I know, I know," I said. She was right. I had given her my word I'd pick the topic over the weekend. I gave my word to Frankie, too, and where had that gotten me?

I went into my room, sat at my desk, and looked at the chart on the wall.

"SCIENCE PROJECT," it said in the space for Monday. I stared at the square. Nothing happened. Then I swiveled in my chair and looked at the other wall. I stared at that for a while. There were no ideas there, either. Only white space. Empty white space.

My brain often doesn't work when I want it to, but now it was definitely on snooze. I knew what the problem was. I was really worried about what happened with Frankie.

Maybe you know the feeling. You've got to think of a topic for your science project, which is due the next day. But you're in a humungous fight with your best friend and you absolutely positively cannot concentrate. I have trouble concentrating when I'm *not* in a fight with anyone, when everything is perfect. It takes a lot of work to focus my brain. But when I have something really big on my mind, it's hopeless.

I stared at the wall some more. The only science project that occurred to me was how to send an electro-wave from my brain to

Frankie's to make him forget that he was mad at me.

I sat there. It seemed like hours went by. I heard my dad and Emily come home. I heard my mom's footsteps in the hall. She was on patrol, circling around to see that I was doing my work. If she was any closer to my bedroom door, she would have been inside. Occasionally, she was, or at least parts of her were. Like her mouth.

"How's it coming?" she asked.

"It's coming," I said.

She casually strolled over to my desk and glanced at my notebook. I had nothing written there. She raised an eyebrow.

"Hey, this takes time, Mom. You can't hurry science. It's not a subject you can speed through."

The truth was that what I kept thinking about was what happened at Aunt Maxine's house. I kept seeing that wall of video equipment with all the numbers and dials and lights flashing at me. I played it over and over in my mind, seeing the television screen with the programs and channels running by, starting at the bottom of the screen and racing to the top. The words and numbers had gone by so fast. If only there had been a way to slow them down. *There must be a million kids like me who can't follow them,* I thought. *I'm not the only slow reader in the world . . . am I? No, no way.*

Wait a minute. Wait just a minute.

That was it! The idea of the century. I'd invent a way to slow down the words and numbers crawling across the television screen. I would be the hero for problem readers around the world.

It was a science project to be proud of. It was the King of All Science Projects. *Hank Zipzer, I love you*, I thought. I sprang up from my chair and danced around my room. I gave myself kisses up and down my arms.

What an idea! What a breakthrough! Way to go, Hank!

CHAPTER 13

AT DINNER THAT NIGHT, I told my mom and dad about my idea. I told them that I was going to find a way to make the program guide on the television screen easy to read for kids like me. I explained that this would help kids around the world and possibly even as far away as Neptune.

"There must be learning challenged kids on Neptune," I said. "I'm sure they need help, too."

"That's a lovely thought, Hank," said my mom. She always tries to help people in need, like giving the leftover food from the deli to the homeless shelter. I could tell she was happy that I was trying to help the learning challenged kids on this and every other planet.

"How exactly are you planning to do this?" asked my father.

"Experimentation, Dad," I said, trying to sound really smart. "The way all science is created."

"Hmmph," my dad grunted. "Sounds messy."

"Do you think Thomas Edison's dad worried that he was making a mess when young Tom invented the lightbulb?" I asked. "No, absolutely not. His dad probably just said, Tom, don't forget to wear gloves so you don't cut yourself on the glass."

"Thomas Edison was thirty-two when he invented the lightbulb in 1879," said my father. "I don't think he was living with his parents at the time."

When you argue with someone who is a crossword puzzle nut, they pull out their facts at the drop of a hat. Someone with facts can be pretty frustrating when you're trying to make a point.

"Oh, you're right, Dad. It was his wife who reminded him about the gloves."

"You're making that up," Emily said through a mouthful of vegetarian lasagna. She pulled a piece of zucchini from the lasagna and handed it to Katherine, who was sitting on her shoulder looking particularly ugly.

"I happen to know that Thomas Edison was very happily married," I said to Emily.

"Oh, yeah? What was his wife's name?"

"Mrs. Edison," I answered.

That made my mom laugh.

"Well, whatever you do," my dad said with a yawn, "make sure you put your name on the paper."

"Thanks for the tip, Dad." I wasn't being sarcastic, either. It was actually a good suggestion since most of the time I forget to put my name on the paper and my teacher Ms. Adolf takes a half point off my grade.

My parents were so tired from the trip that they went to bed right after dinner.

"Don't stay up too late," my mom said, giving me a kiss. "Tomorrow's a school day." Like I could forget something like that.

I went to my room and tried to write a few notes about my science topic. The more I thought about my invention, the more excited I got about it. I even picked up the phone to call Frankie and tell him my idea. But then I remembered that he wasn't speaking to me. That made me sad, because when you have a best friend, you want to be able to tell him when you have a good idea.

In a couple of minutes, I heard my dad snoring from his room. Then I heard my mom click off her reading light.

I got up and headed for the living room. I needed to check out the cable box to see if I could figure out how it controlled the speed of the words on the TV screen. This was going to take some serious investigation.

Cheerio was asleep on my bed. He lifted his head and started to wag his tail. Sometimes that means "I love you" but most of the time that means "I'm about to go nuts and start chasing my tail and spin around like a top." I needed his cooperation so I could work without being disturbed.

"Stay, boy," I whispered.

I took my pillow and put it gently under his head. Cheerio loves to sleep on my pillow or my clothes or anything that smells like me. You gotta love him.

I went out into the hall and the floor

creaked. I froze in my tracks and counted to twenty-seven. My dad was still snoring, and there was no light coming from under my parents' door, so I figured it was okay to go on. When I reached the living room, I could move around more freely because the carpet covered the sound of my footsteps.

I picked up the cable box that sits on top of the TV. I couldn't see it very well. The outside told me nothing about how it worked. That meant one thing. I was going to have to go inside the box. It was Thomas Edison time.

I tried to separate the top and bottom of the box with my fingernail, but there was no way to get the cover off without a screwdriver. We keep our tools in a red metal toolbox under the kitchen sink. Quietly, I crept into the kitchen, found the toolbox, and opened it. I picked out a small screwdriver with a grooved end called a Phillips head screwdriver.

Suddenly, the kitchen light came on. I spun around, and there was Emily with Katherine perched on her shoulder.

"What are you doing with that?" Emily demanded, eyeing the screwdriver in my hand.

"Stuff," I answered.

"What kind of stuff?"

"Science stuff."

"What kind of science stuff?"

"Emily," I said. "When I want you to know, I'll tell you."

"What's the big secret?"

"What are *you* doing up?" I asked her. If she could play twenty questions, so could I.

"I'm worried about Katherine," she said. "She's acting strange."

"Of course she's acting strange," I said. "She's your iguana."

Katherine looked at me, shot her tongue out, and hissed so loud it sounded like air gushing out of a tire. She even lifted her lip—or at least where her lip would be if she had lips—and flashed her teeth. That *was* strange. Katherine's usually in a pretty good mood, at least as far as iguana moods go.

"She keeps pacing back and forth across the room like she's nervous," Emily said. "I think she had a nightmare."

"Maybe they had *The Mutant Moth That Ate Toledo* on at the pet store, and it gave her the creeps," I said.

There it was again, just when I thought I had stopped thinking about it. Obviously, I had mutant moths on the brain.

"Is Frankie still mad at you?" Emily asked.

"Big-time."

"Do you want to talk about it?" Emily was trying to be nice. "Katherine and I are very good listeners, aren't we, Kathy?" She nuzzled Katherine.

"That's okay," I said. "You and Katherine go to sleep. She needs her beauty rest."

Emily started to leave, then she turned around. "I think Katherine would like a nuzzle from you," she said. "It would make her feel loved."

Oh brother, the things a guy has to do to get a little privacy around here. I reached out and gave Katherine a pat on the head. She hissed and flashed her teeth at me again. That's gratitude for you.

I decided to take the cable box into my room so I could work on it in private. I disconnected the box from the TV, which wasn't hard. I took it in my room and sat down. I noticed that there were four screws holding the top to the bottom. I unscrewed them and put them on the floor.

No, Hank, I thought. *You are going to lose these if you leave them here, and then you'll never be able to put the box back together again.*

I got up and put all four screws in a little plastic box I keep in my desk drawer. I usually keep my special clear marbles in there, but I took those out and put them into another compartment.

I jiggled the top of the cable box, and it came off very easily. Wow, things were going well.

When I lifted the top off, the inside was not at all what I expected. It was jammed with circuit boards and microchips and lots of wires tangled up together.

I took everything out of the box and separated the pieces, laying all the parts down on my rug. There sure were a lot of parts. I got so involved taking the box apart and inspecting every single piece that I lost all track of time. The next time I looked up, two hours had gone by. That happens a lot to me. Either I can't focus at all, or I focus so hard I shut everything else out.

Suddenly, I heard a toilet flush, then footsteps. They were coming toward my room!

"Hank?" my dad whispered from the hall. "What are you doing up?"

I had to do something fast. I knew he'd come in, and my dad is not the kind of person who would be happy to see his cable box in a million pieces on my floor. I don't know your dad, but I bet he's not that kind of person, either.

I flung myself down on the rug so my body covered all the parts. I heard a couple of things crunch under my butt. There was no time to check them out. I barely had enough time to hit the ground before my dad opened the door.

"Hey, Dad," I said, in a very casual voice, like I always stay up until midnight on a school night lying around on my rug. "What's up?"

"You are," he said. "Go to bed."

"Thanks for the suggestion," I said, "but I'm not all that sleepy."

"Head on pillow, Hank. Now."

"Okay, Dad. I'll be in bed in one second."

He clicked the door shut. I could tell he was

standing outside, waiting for my lights to go off. I scooped up all the parts of the cable box in my hands.

"N-O-W," came my father's voice, as he spelled out the word. When my father spells out words, that is a clue he means business.

"Right n-o-w, Dad," I spelled back.

I opened my desk drawer and quickly tossed all the pieces in. Chips, circuits, wires, and other parts scattered everywhere. I kicked the top and bottom of the cable box under my bed and hopped under the covers just as my dad turned the doorknob and stuck his head inside.

"Sleep fast," he whispered. "It's late."

"I'm trying, Dad, but someone keeps opening my door."

He left, and I tried to close my eyes, but all I could see in my head were the bits and pieces of the cable box crammed in my top drawer. I had a bad feeling that box was never going to come together in the same way again.

CHAPTER 14

I MUST HAVE FINALLY fallen asleep, because my dad's voice woke me early the next morning.

"Out of bed, Hank. Breakfast in five," he called, knocking on my door.

Usually, it takes several warnings to get me out of bed, but I jumped up and yelled back, "I'm way ahead of you, Dad." I went to my desk drawer and pulled it open. Nothing had changed overnight. The chips and circuit boards and wires were lying there exactly as I had left them the night before. How come in fairy tales, magic elves arrive in the night and put everything back the way it was? I ask you, where are those elves when a guy needs them?

I imagined the punishment that would come down on me if my dad saw that mess. My dad always says the punishment should fit the crime, and I had a horrible feeling my punishment for taking away *his* television would be that he'd take away *mine*, whenever it was finally working again.

"No TV for a month," he'd say. Or maybe even, "No TV for a year." My head spun! I had to get that cable box fixed before he found out about it.

I was safe for a while, because no one in my family turns on the TV until the nighttime. But at six thirty every night, my Dad watches the nightly news, followed by *Hollywood Squares*. I'm not too good at math, but I figured I had something like twelve hours to get our cable up and running.

But how?

I didn't need magic elves. I needed Frankie Townsend. If anyone could put that box back together, it was Frankie. He is a boy genius with electronic stuff. I happen to know firsthand that he's had a subscription to *Popular Electronics* since he was eight years old. And he reads it, too. Cover to cover.

I thought about my situation at breakfast. I had to find a way to apologize to Frankie that he'd accept. I needed him to help me fix the cable box by the time my father plopped in his chair and flicked on the nightly news.

After breakfast, I raced into my room to get my backpack, but before I left, I took out a piece of paper.

"KEEP OUT!" I wrote. "SIENSE PROJECT IN PROGES."

I don't think I spelled too many of the words right, but it got the message across, just in case my dad or anyone else felt like snooping.

I taped the sign on my door, and closed it tight. I considered pointing out the sign to my dad, but I really didn't need to. My dad is a major-league sign reader. All you have to do is walk down Amsterdam Avenue with him and he will read every sign he sees—*out loud.*

"Harvey's Pizza—a dollar a slice. Kim's Korean Market, fresh roses today. Big Apple Laundromat, Free Dry with Wash. Manhattan Bagels, two free when you buy a dozen." His sign reading habit was great when I was a little guy and couldn't read. But now that I'm older, it's pretty annoying. And now Emily's starting to do it, too. Maybe there's a gene for annoying oral sign reading. I hope I don't pass it on to my kids.

"I'll meet you downstairs, Dad," I called. He was walking us to school, but I wanted to get down there early and see if I could talk to Frankie before we set out.

When I got to the lobby, only Ashley and Robert were there.

"Where's Frankie?" I asked. "We've got to talk. I'm going to buzz his apartment."

"Hank," Ashley said, stopping me from going back inside. "Frankie already left. He didn't want to walk with us."

"He's still that mad?" I gulped.

"I don't know," Ashley answered. "He just took off with his dad."

"Listen, Ashley, we've got to figure out how to get Frankie to talk to me again."

"Give him a day or two, he'll get over it," she said.

"I don't have that much time," I said. "I need him now. He's got to help me fix my cable box—by tonight."

"I can fix a cable box," said Robert.

"Can you really?" I asked him.

"Sure," he said. "Call the cable company and ask for a new one." Then he laughed.

Great, *now* Robert was developing a sense of humor. Just when I needed him to be the nerd he's always been, he's turned into Captain Wisecrack.

"Actually," he said, "anyone can get a new box. My mom just got one for the TV in her room."

It was the perfect solution. I'd call the cable company right after school and ask them to bring over a new box.

My dad and Emily arrived downstairs with Cheerio on a leash. When it's my dad's day to walk us to school, he always brings Cheerio along for the exercise. He likes to sniff the sidewalk and curbs—Cheerio, that is, not my dad. We headed down Amsterdam Avenue, and I was already feeling much better. It's great when you find a solution to a problem. It's like someone has lifted a huge sack of potatoes off your back.

"Robert," I whispered. "You're an all right guy, even if you do wear a white shirt and tie to school every day."

He reached out with his scrawny little arm and threw me a fake punch in the arm. Boy, is that kid weak.

"By the way, buddy," he said, "It costs fifty-eight dollars."

"What does?"

"The cable box. Actually, fifty-eight dollars and forty cents."

"Robert, why didn't you tell me this before?"

"You didn't ask."

"But I only have ten dollars," I said. "That means I'm thirty-eight dollars and forty cents short."

"Make that *forty* eight dollars and forty cents," Robert said.

In case you haven't noticed, my math isn't any better than my spelling.

This was not looking good for the future of my television privileges.

CHAPTER 15

WHEN WE REACHED SCHOOL, I saw Frankie standing outside on the steps. I went charging up to him and launched into my apology.

"Frankie! Listen, I've been thinking about what happened and I've got to tell you that—"

Before I could even finish my sentence, Nick McKelty appeared on the steps next to us. Nick McKelty doesn't care if you're in the middle of an apology. He just blurts out whatever he has to say, which is usually something loud and obnoxious. Correction. It is *always* something loud and obnoxious.

"Hey, Townsend," he hollered at Frankie, not even paying the slightest attention to me. "What did you think of *The Mutant Moth That Ate Toledo.* Was I right or was I right?"

"I wouldn't know," Frankie answered, giving me a dark stare. "I missed it."

"Don't tell me you didn't see it?" McKelty said, his big mouth hanging open in surprise. "The part where the moth ate the policeman's guts and grew to the size of an apartment building was awesome. A total gross-out."

"I wish I had seen it," Frankie said quietly, staring at me until I thought his brown eyes were going to pop out of their sockets. "Someone I know was supposed to tape it for me."

McKelty, who is generally not the brightest bulb in the lamp, put two and two together for the first time in his life.

"Hey, sounds like Zipzer screwed up again." He smirked. "What did you do, Zipper Face? Forget what the ON button looks like?"

I must have looked like someone punched me in the stomach. McKelty saw me flinch. He could tell he had found a sore spot, and now he was going to go for the knockout.

"Yeah, those ON and OFF buttons are really hard to push," he said, putting his huge face right up to mine. His breath was like a dragon who had eaten six onions for breakfast.

"Back off, McKelty." I could only take so

much. "This is none of your business."

McKelty grinned, and I noticed he still had some of his breakfast lodged in that big space between his two front teeth. I'm guessing it was waffles, but I couldn't entirely rule out cinnamon toast.

"Did I tell you girls that my dad is getting the original poster of *The Mutant Moth* movie for me," he bragged. "Not a copy, either, but the only one they ever made."

There it was. The McKelty factor at work. That guy exaggerates everything. We call it truth times one hundred.

"And did I mention that it's signed by the moth himself?" he said, blasting me with another giant dose of his dragon breath.

"What'd he do, sign it in wing dust?" I shot back.

Frankie laughed. That was a good sign.

"You're funny, Zipzer," said Nick. "Retarded, but funny."

Ordinarily, if he hadn't been so mad at me, Frankie would have jumped to my defense. But he didn't say a word. He just pulled his Yankees hat down over his eyes, so he wouldn't have to look at me. McKelty sensed that Frankie wasn't talking, so he fired off another insult.

"Listen, zippety zipper man. Maybe you can come over sometime and I'll teach you how to work a VCR. Oh, and when we're done with that, I'll teach you how to tie your shoelaces. I remember you had trouble with that in kindergarten. You were never too swift, were you, pal?"

"That's enough, McKelty," Frankie said.

Yes! Frankie had spoken! I hoped that meant that he wasn't mad anymore.

Before I could find out, Principal Love came out onto the steps. Actually, I heard him before I saw him appear. You can't mistake the squeak, squeak, squeak of his Velcro sneakers. He's the only grown man I know who wears white Velcro sneakers with a navy blue suit and tie. Maybe he had trouble learning to tie his shoes in kindergarten like I did.

Principal Love started to gather up the kids who were still standing around.

"Everybody inside," he said in his voice that sounds like he's on the public address system, even without a microphone. "You know what I always say—a classroom without students is like a bird without a song."

Principal Love says things that almost make sense, but then when you think about them, don't make any sense at all. What's even worse is that he likes to say these things twice.

"Mr. Zipzer," he said, pointing at me. "Are you on your way to class?"

Before I could answer, Nick butted right in. "*I* am, sir, and I'm looking forward to school today."

The one true thing you can say about Nick McKelty is that he never, ever misses an opportunity to suck up.

Principal Love gave Nick a friendly slap on the back. "Yes, sirree, a classroom without students is like a bird without a song."

Frankie and I bolted for the door and headed upstairs, trying like crazy not to have to walk with Nick McKelty. It wasn't a problem, though. He was hanging back with Principal Love, trying to score a few extra points.

"Nick's probably telling him how much he enjoys his announcements on the loudspeaker," I said.

Frankie almost laughed as we took off up the stairs.

"Does this mean we're okay again?" I asked.

"I'm thinking about it," Frankie said.

"Well, can you think about it fast, because I'm calling an emergency meeting after school. Four o'clock, in the club house. I really need you there."

"What's up?" Frankie asked.

"I can't even begin to explain to you what a pickle I've gotten myself into."

"Give me a hint." I had gotten him curious at least.

"Imagine your cable box."

"Got it."

"Now imagine it in, let's say, fifty pieces."

"Got it."

"I got it, too. And it's under my bed."

"You didn't."

"Oh, yes I did."

"Zip, is there anything you don't screw up?" Frankie said as he reached the top of the stairs.

Ouch.

CHAPTER 16

ZIP-ZER! ZIP-ZER! ZIP-ZER! ZIP-ZER!

BEFORE I COULD SAY ANYTHING MORE, we were outside our classroom. Ms. Adolf was waiting by the door.

Some teachers say good morning when you come in. Some even read you a chapter of a story before you get to work. But not Ms. Adolf. No, she believes in getting right down to business.

As soon as the bell rang, she took off the silver key she wears on a lanyard around her neck and unlocked her desk drawer. Inside that drawer is where she keeps her roll book, which is her favorite thing in the world. Ms. Adolf took out her roll book, a red pencil, and—you guessed it—got right down to business.

"Pupils," she said. "Today your science project topics are due. Who would like to go first?"

Heather Payne's hand shot up in the air.

"Me! Me!" She begged. She waved her hand right under Ms. Adolf's nose and grunted "Me! Me!" another seven or eight times. Heather can't stand it if she doesn't go first. I bet there's someone like that in your class, too.

Heather said for her project she would be taking photographs to show the effects of regular flossing on gum disease. Personally, I'd rather repeat fourth grade twenty times than take pictures of gum disease. But I guess that's why Heather Payne got straight As on her last report card and I got four Ds.

Hector Ruiz said he was going to build a rain forest out of toothpicks, plastic flowers, and real leaves. Kim Paulson was studying fingernail polish and its drying time in various climates. Ms. Adolf raised an eyebrow, but agreed to it when Kim explained how she planned to relate nail polish drying to the evaporation cycle. Frankie was going to build a radio from a kit he sent away for from an ad in *Popular Electronics*. Ashley was planning to make a model of the human kidney from kitchen sponges. Luke Whitman was going to do his project on tarantulas. He owns one named Mel. Mel has very hairy legs.

Then came my turn.

"Originally, I was going to study the tummy sliding habits of penguins," I began, "because penguins look so extremely cute when they slide on their stomachs."

Everyone in the class laughed, even though I was totally serious.

"However, I've changed my mind," I went on.

"That was a wise decision, Henry," said Ms. Adolf. She always calls me Henry, even though I've begged her to call me Hank. Ms. Adolf doesn't approve of nicknames.

"I plan to invent a device that will help slow readers follow the written words on the television screen as they speed along their merry way."

I paused to let the full, wonderful effect of my idea seep into Ms. Adolf's brain.

"What are you talking about, Henry?" she sighed.

"I'm getting to that," I said, trying not to panic.

"Please hurry."

"Remember Thomas Edison?" I said, talking

fast now. "He invented the lightbulb. Why? Because he probably couldn't see well enough to read in the dark and if he had moved closer to the candle, he might have set his hair on fire."

Ms. Adolf tapped her foot impatiently. She was wearing gray shoes to match the gray clothes she always wears, which match her gray face. "Henry, what is your point?"

"My point is that the best inventions happen out of need. And I really, really, really need to be able to read what's on the program guide on television."

"What you need is a brain that works!" hollered Nick the Tick from the back of the room.

"He's laughing now, Ms. Adolf," I said, "but when I'm a famous inventor, he'll be wishing he was me. Challenged readers around the globe will be chanting my name."

With that, Luke Whitman started to chant. It doesn't take much to get Luke started.

"ZIP-ZER! ZIP-ZER! ZIP-ZER!"

Ryan Shimazato joined in and so did his pals Ricky and Justin. They did everything he did.

"ZIP-ZER! ZIP-ZER! ZIP-ZER!"

Then Kim Paulson and Katie Sperling and Hector Ruiz started to chant. Ashley piped up and Frankie did, too. Even Heather Payne got on board. Pretty soon, the entire class except for—you got it—McKelty the Pelty was chanting my name.

"ZIP-ZER! ZIP-ZER! ZIP-ZER!"

I had told Ms. Adolf that one day my invention was going to make the Zipzer name famous. See, it was starting already.

CHAPTER 17

FRANKIE KEPT TO HIMSELF the rest of the day. He was still ignoring me when his mom came to school to walk us home. She teaches yoga, so she's really good at sensing when people are stressed.

"I'm feeling a negative energy flow," she said.

No kidding.

I was deep in thought. The way I figured it, I had Plan A and Plan B. For Plan A, I would buy a new cable box. But since I didn't have the money or the time to earn it, I moved on to Plan B. Plan B meant I had to rebuild the cable box in two hours without Frankie's help. That wasn't much more likely to happen than Plan A, but it was the only hope I had.

Ashley was working on blowing spit bubbles and launching them into the air, which kept her tongue too busy to talk. Ashley is always working on a new body trick to add to her collection, which includes tying a cherry stem into a knot using only her tongue and wiggling her eyebrows and ears at the same time.

"Maybe we should do some anti-stress breathing as we walk," Mrs. Townsend suggested.

So all the way down 78th Street and across Amsterdam Avenue we took deep deep breaths in through our noses and exhaled our stress out through our mouths. A couple of times I choked on the taxi fumes and by the time we got to our building, I was feeling a little light-headed.

"Don't forget the emergency meeting," I whispered to Ashley and Frankie as we got into the elevator. "Four o'clock in the clubhouse."

"I'll be there," answered Robert. That kid has hearing like a bat.

"I need you there," I said to Frankie.

He got out on his floor without saying a word.

A few minutes before four, I rode the elevator down to the basement and was waiting at the clubhouse at four o'clock sharp. I sat down on one of Mrs. Fink's cardboard boxes. This one was labeled LONG UNDERWEAR. When I saw that, I jumped up and decided I'd rather stand.

Ashley arrived next. She had changed out of her school clothes and was wearing a hat that said THINKING CAP across the front in pink rhinestones. She glued the rhinestones on herself, like she does on most of her clothes.

"I've got my thinking cap on," she said proudly.

"That's good, Ash. I'm going to need all the thoughts I can get."

I heard footsteps coming down the hall. I was hoping it would be Frankie, but it turned out to be Robert. He had changed out of his school clothes, too, which meant he still had on his white starchy shirt but had taken his tie off. Robert goes casual.

We waited for five minutes more. Frankie still wasn't there.

"I guess he's not coming," Ashley said. She sounded truly sad.

I wondered how Frankie could let me down like this in my time of need? Then I realized that I had let him down, too.

I had to face the fact that Frankie wasn't going to be there.

"The purpose of this meeting," I began, "is to see if we can find a way to rebuild my cable box before my dad finds out I took it apart and takes away my television privileges for life. Does anyone have any ideas?"

"I do," said a voice from out in the hall.

I didn't need to even look. I'd know that voice in my sleep.

Frankie Townsend, are you a hero or what!!

I tried not to scream and yell and jump up and slap him on the back two thousand times.

"Man, am I glad to see you!" I said to Frankie. I have never spoken seven words I meant more.

"You got a screwdriver, Mr. Fix It?" Frankie asked.

"A whole box of them."

"Then what are you waiting for?" he said.

"You," I answered. "I was waiting for you."

CHAPTER 18

WE DIDN'T HAVE MUCH TIME, but with Frankie back on the team, at least there was hope. We raced into the elevator and headed for my apartment.

"Thanks for showing up," I said to him as we watched the floor numbers change above the elevator doors.

"I owed it to you," said Frankie.

"Why?"

"I realized you got yourself into this mess for me. That's why you took that cable box apart—because you felt bad about screwing up the movie, and you never wanted that to happen again. Am I right?"

"Yeah," I said. "And now look. I've screwed up again. Hank Zipzer, world's greatest screwup."

"But we love you anyway," Ashley said.

"Speak for yourself, Ashweena," Frankie said with a laugh.

When we walked into my apartment, my dad and Emily were crawling around the floor on their hands and knees. They were looking under all the furniture and in back of the bookcases.

"We have a problem," Emily said. "Katherine is missing again."

"So what's the problem?" I asked.

"That is so not funny, Hank," said Emily. "I'm worried."

"Maybe you just nuzzled her one time too many," I said.

"Hank, this is important to Emily," my dad said. "Not everything's a joke."

"You're right, Dad," I said. "Emily, I'm very sorry you have a missing iguana. Now if you'll excuse us, we're going to my room. Come on, guys."

We headed for my bedroom—everyone except Robert, that is.

"I'd help you look for her, but I'm allergic to dust," Robert said to Emily. "Actually, it's not the dust I'm allergic to, but the dust mites.

They're tiny bugs that infect my sinus cavities causing green mucus."

"Robert, my man," Frankie said. "You're grossing us out."

"I don't mind hearing about it," said Emily. "I get sinus congestion, too."

I tell you, Robert and Emily were made for each other. Two nose-blowing, iguana-loving peas in a pod.

Robert followed us into my bedroom and closed the door. By then, I had pulled open the top drawer and was showing Frankie the pieces of the cable box. Frankie picked up two of the circuit boards. He laid them next to each other on the desktop, and moved them around until they clicked into place. Then he did the same thing with two more pieces and attached a couple of wires.

I had moved those pieces around for hours, and nothing had happened.

"This isn't so bad, Zip," Frankie said. "I think old Humpty Dumpty can put this baby back together again."

Frankie sat down at my desk to work. Ashley and I handed him the pieces one by one, and he put them together. Robert was his assistant, and I have to admit, he did a pretty good job.

We were halfway finished assembling the box when I heard the door to my room being pushed open. I must not have closed it all the way.

"Emily," I said, without looking up. "The sign says PRIVATE."

"That's not Emily," Robert said. His voice sounded strange, kind of freaked out.

I looked over toward the entrance and couldn't believe my eyes. A pair of my father's boxer shorts was opening the door and walking into my room. The underpants crossed my bedroom floor and disappeared under my bed.

"Did you guys see what I saw?" Ashley said.

"Mutant underwear," said Frankie. "It had legs."

I scrunched down and looked under my bed. There were the underpants, lying inside the plastic shell of the cable box. Surrounding my father's boxers were a bunch of other objects— three cotton balls, one of my mom's furry slippers, a whole bunch of crumpled-up toilet paper, and, I hate to say it, a pair of tighty-whitey Ninja underpants that had once belonged to yours truly.

I stuck my hand under the bed and tried to pull out the cable box so I could get a closer look. No sooner had I touched the box than a loud hissing filled the room. It was coming from my father's boxers! I am not kidding. His underpants were hissing.

A long gray tongue shot out from one of the leg holes of the boxers.

"They're alive!" Ashley screamed.

The tongue disappeared, then a snout came out, followed by a lizardy face.

"Katherine!" I said. "What are you doing in there?"

Katherine tossed the boxers off her head, and started pushing them under her body where the other soft objects were.

I reached out for Katherine, and she hissed at me like I was her worst enemy.

"What's wrong with you?" I asked.

"I'll get Emily," Ashley said. "She'll know."

Ashley returned in a second with Emily.

"Close the door so Dad won't come in," I

told Emily.

I was standing in front of the cable box. I didn't want Emily to see what was going on until I could prepare her for the sight.

"I have good news and bad news," I said to Emily. "The good news is we found Katherine. The bad news is . . . we found Katherine."

"Let me see her," Emily demanded. I stepped aside. She looked at Katherine, who was sitting in the cable box on top of the pile of underwear, cotton balls, slippers, and toilet paper. Emily stared at Katherine for a long while, and I couldn't tell if she was going to laugh or cry. Then she broke into a huge smile.

"Do you know what this means?" she asked me.

"Yes," I said. "Your lizard is having a nervous breakdown."

"Katherine is trying to tell us something," Emily said.

"What? That she wants to wear men's underwear?"

"No, silly," said Emily. "I think Katherine is building a nest. For her babies."

I thought for sure my head was going to

blow right off.

"Oh no she isn't! No babies. Not in my cable box!" I said, getting a little panicked.

"Hank, you're going to be a big brother." Emily was practically crying with joy. "And I'm going to be a big sister, aren't I, Kathy?" She reached out to give Katherine a nuzzle. Katherine hissed and showed her teeth, which should teach Emily to never touch an iguana in underpants.

"She's going to be such a good mama," Emily said.

"I want that lizard out of that box," I said. "As a matter of fact, out of my room. Come on, Katherine. You're going bye-bye."

I reached for Katherine. She was just going to have to find another place to be pregnant. But when my hand got close to her, she hissed at me louder than before. That iguana meant business.

"She can't be moved," said Emily. "She might even attack you."

"Emily's right," said Ashley. "I've read that you can never come between a mother and her babies."

"Well, everybody listen up," I said. "I DO NOT, repeat, DO NOT want a baby iguana hatching in my room!"

"You're not going to have one iguana," said Robert. "Iguanas lay between eighteen and forty-five eggs at a time."

I thought my ears were playing tricks on me. "Robert. Are you telling me that Katherine could have forty-five baby iguanas tucked away in those underpants?" I asked.

"Yes," said Robert.

"Isn't it a miracle?" said Emily.

A miracle? Had she lost whatever little bit of a mind she once had?

This was no miracle. This was a disaster.

CHAPTER 19

LET'S ALL AGREE right now that I am a total knucklehead. I had caused a problem the size of Australia, and as far as I could see, there was no solution. I mean, how do you get a hissing, pregnant iguana out of your cable box?

We sat in my room discussing the problem, and we all came up with the same answer. You cannot get a pregnant iguana out of your cable box. Never has been done. Never will be done.

So we had to move to Plan B, which was formerly known as Plan A. Since Katherine was going to stay in the cable box to hatch her eggs, which, by the way, takes ninety days, the only solution was to get a new cable box. We would have to do this before my dad found out that I had trashed ours. Magik 3's job was to help me get the box, and Emily's job was to keep her mouth shut about it.

I stared at Katherine curled up in her nest, and wondered about two questions. How do iguanas get pregnant anyway? And why do these kinds of strange things always happen to me?

"Zip, snap out of it, will you, dude? We don't have time to daydream," Frankie yelled almost in my ear.

"I'm not daydreaming. I'm day nightmaring." I answered.

"Did you hear what we said?" said Ashley. "We have to get the cable company's number before they close."

"Maybe they can deliver a new box right away," Frankie said.

I looked at my watch. It was five thirty. One hour until my dad would be turning on the nightly news. I sped out of my bedroom and slid down the hallway linoleum around the corner into the kitchen. It's good to know you can still have fun even in very bad situations.

My mom keeps all the important numbers and business cards taped to the kitchen wall, which is canary yellow, by the way. There are notes with scribbled numbers all around the phone. Because I was so stressed, I couldn't focus. All the cards and Post-Its with numbers started to blur. One of them had the number of the cable company, but I couldn't tell which one. I couldn't find it in the sea of cards.

"Here, you guys look," I said, rubbing my eyes.

"Let me do it," said Robert, moving Ashley aside. "I'm the calmest."

"You're also the shortest, Robert," Frankie said. "Ashweena, you take that part of the wall and I'll look on this side."

"Here it is! Here it is!" Ashley screamed.

My heart started to beat really fast. How can you be so happy just finding a phone number? When your life, social and otherwise, depends on it, that's how.

"No, no. This is a cable-knit sweater company," she said. "Sorry, guys. Keep looking."

As always, Frankie was the man. He took a bright green card down from the wall.

"Here it is," he said. "Coxy Cable. Okay, Zip, start dialing."

"Read it slowly, Frankie. I can't keep all the

numbers in my head at once," I said.

"362," Frankie started.

"362," I said, punching the numbers. "Go on."

"5555," Frankie continued. "Got that? Four fives."

"5545," I said.

"Go slow, Hank. Five, five, five, five," he repeated.

"Oh, okay. I got that. It's ringing. Shhhh."

"Thank you for calling Coxy Cable," said a recorded voice on the other end. "Please listen carefully to the following menu."

"Here," I said, pushing the receiver into Ashley's hands. "You do it."

Ash listened for a while and pushed the number 3. She listened for another while and said, "Here. Someone said hello." She handed me back the phone.

"Hello. How are you today?" I didn't wait for an answer. "My name is Hank Zipzer. My parents are Randi and Stanley Zipzer and they are customers. Good ones. Please, we need a new box by six o'clock today. You're not going to believe what happened. My sister's idiotic

113

iguana got a Phillips screwdriver, opened the box, and filled it with boxer shorts. Now she's laying eggs in it. Can you believe that?"

I finally took a breath.

"No," the operator answered.

"You can't?" I answered. "Well, I know it's totally amazing. Anyway, I need to watch a Discovery Kids show for an assignment and it starts at six today. So please, can you come? Please, please, oh please?"

"I'm sorry," the operator said.

"Don't say that!" I interrupted her. "I asked you so nicely not to say that."

Robert couldn't stand it anymore. "What did she say?" he asked.

"They can't bring a box today or tonight!" I said. "We're dead meat."

I slid down the wall and held my head in my hands. Ashley took the phone back and asked when was the earliest they could bring a box.

She covered the mouthpiece and asked me when someone would be home.

"I'll be here after school tomorrow," I answered. "Ask her how much it costs for a new box."

"Excuse me, madam, may I inquire how much a new cable box will be?" Ashley asked.

She covered the mouth piece again and whispered, "Fifty-eight dollars and forty cents."

"I told you that's what it would cost," said Robert.

"Where am I going to get that kind of money?" I asked.

"I'm in for ten bucks," Ashley said.

"Me, too," Frankie said.

"I've got twenty-three dollars and forty cents," said Robert.

"I can't take all your money, Robert," I said.

"It's a loan," said Robert. "You can pay me back from your Magik 3 earnings."

"You're a good man," Frankie said to him, and slapped him on the back. Poor Robert went flying across the kitchen. "A little man, but a good man."

Ashley was adding up the numbers.

"You're still five dollars short," she whispered.

"Just tell them to come as soon as they can," I whispered back. "Maybe we can get Emily to cough it up."

I happen to know that Emily has a wad of birthday money stashed in a fake 7 UP can in her room. When Papa Pete gives me money for my birthday, I always spend it the minute I get it. But not Emily. She hides it away in that can like a little squirrel. She says she's saving for a snake. Either that or an armadillo.

Ashley made the arrangements. They told us the cable guy would be at our apartment between 3:30 and 5:15 the next day. My mom would still be at The Crunchy Pickle, but if I could find a way to get my father out of the house, they'd replace the box without him seeing it.

That could work. There was only one small problem left.

We were less than an hour away from the nightly news, which, as you know, is my father's TV time.

So I ask you.

WHAT WAS I GOING TO DO WITH MY DAD TONIGHT?!?!?!?

CHAPTER 20

THE ANSWER CAME to me in eight letters. S-C-R-A-B-B-L-E.

I'm sure I've told you before that my father loves crossword puzzles. As a matter of fact, he's a word fanatic. He loves letters and words no matter where they are. Sometimes he reads the dictionary just for fun. He's got about five of them placed all over the house for easy access. He has one next to his bed, one on the living room coffee table. He even has one next to the toilet.

A game of Scrabble is *his* idea of the perfect evening. It's *my* idea of torture. Trying to put a bunch of wooden tiles with letters into words— long words that have to be spelled right—well, let me just say, this is a major KEEP OUT sign for me. The only time a game of Scrabble is fun for me is when it's in its box with the cover on.

My dad and Emily play Scrabble a lot. Sometimes my mom joins in, too. The three of them laugh and argue for hours about whether "xeric" is a word or not. They used to invite me to play, but I am such a spelling moron that they stopped asking me. That's actually fine with me, because playing always embarrasses me anyway.

But when you're trying to keep your father from watching TV because you've taken apart his cable box, you'll do anything. Even make a fool of yourself in a Scrabble game.

After dinner, at the moment when my dad usually sits down for his dose of nightly news and *Hollywood Squares,* I sprang it on him.

"Hey, Dad, let's play a game of good old Scrabble."

At first, my dad couldn't believe it.

"Are you joking with me, Hank?"

"No, you always want me to play with you and I was thinking we could share a little quality spelling time together. As a matter of fact, I hear the game calling out to me now. *Hank, isn't this the perfect time to pull me off the shelf?*"

"You're a nut, Hank." My father laughed. "But I've never said no to a game of Scrabble in my life. Emily!" he called out. "Want to play some Scrabble with us?"

"No thanks, Dad," she answered. "Kathy and I are just talking about girl stuff."

Emily was in my room, watching over Katherine. I let her stay in there for as long as she wanted in exchange for not spilling the beans about el cable boxo. We hadn't told my parents Katherine's baby news yet. We had decided to wait until the new cable box was in, to be sure there would be no questions asked.

My mom didn't want to play, either, because she was in the kitchen experimenting with a new recipe. I think it was tofu chips that are supposed to taste like potato chips but actually taste like cement. Not that I've eaten cement, but I imagine it tastes like her tofu chips.

So it was my dad and me sitting down at the Scrabble board. We set it up on the dining room table and each took seven letters from the pile. My dad let me go first. I stared at those tiles, but I didn't see any words there. I squinted up my eyes. Still nothing. Then, you're not going to believe it, I saw a word! Right there under my nose!

Hey, Scrabble wasn't so difficult.

I picked up my tiles and put them down on the board so hard they made that snapping sound. There it was! My word!

"N–O." I spelled it out proudly. "No."

"That's your word?" my father asked.

"Isn't it unbelievable, Dad? My first try and I got two points. And you thought I couldn't play Scrabble!"

"Hank, the goal is to get as many points as possible."

"I'm on my way, Dad. I'm on my way."

It was my dad's turn. He stared at his tiles, running his hands through his hair, which is pretty messy to begin with.

"Hmmmm," he said, which made him sound like he was concentrating really hard. I made a note to make that sound during my next turn.

Suddenly, his face lit up and he looked at me with a big grin. He took all seven of his letters—that's right, *all* of them—and laid them out underneath my N.

"N-E-R-V-A-T-I-O-N," he said, as he put down each letter.

"Is that a word?" I asked.

"It's a system of nerves. Look it up," he said, pushing the dictionary toward me.

"It's okay," I said, pushing the dictionary back toward him. "I believe you."

I was feeling like a system of nerves myself. It was my turn again. It had just been my turn, and here it was again.

I stared at the letters on the board, then at the ones in my hand. The tiles began to look like they were swimming in an ocean. The letters became sharks about to attack me. I wanted to get away from them more than anything.

"Come on, Hank. Go."

A word. Think of a word. I can't think of a word. I'm wordless.

Come on, Hank. You must know some word. How am I feeling? I'm feeling tense. Tense. It starts with a T. There's a T on the board. Okay, Hank. Way to go.

I picked up four letters from my hand and placed them next to the T on the board.

"T-E-N-C-E," I said proudly. "How many

points is that, Dad?"

"None yet, Hank. That's not a word."

"Sure it is. As in nervous. You know."

"Oh," my dad said. "Tense. Do you have an S?"

"No. Why?"

"Because tense, the way you're using it, is spelled with an S. T-E-N-S-E."

"Oh," I said. I took the letters off the board and put them back on my tray. I stared at the board again. Then I saw an amazing opportunity.

"This is going to make your socks go up and down," I said to my dad.

I started with the "I" in "nervation," and built this word around it.

"A-I-N-M-A-L."

"What does that spell?" my father asked.

"Animal," I said. "As in tiger, anteater, iguana. And do not ask me to spell any of those."

My father looked at the board, then at me.

"Hank, what are the first three letters in animal?"

I sounded it out, then answered. "A-N-I," I said.

"Do you see that you flipped those letters around on the board?"

"No," I said. "How many points, Dad?"

"You really can't see that you spelled the word wrong?"

I looked at the board. The letters looked okay to me.

"No, I'm not kidding with you."

My mother had come out of the kitchen and was standing in the doorway watching us. My father looked over at her.

"He really can't see it," he said.

"That's what they've been saying at school, honey," my mom said. "This is one of his problem areas."

Hello! Ding dong! That's what I'd been telling them ever since the subject of spelling first came up. I can't do it. I try and I try, but my brain just won't picture the words. I know my letters but they won't go into words. Or at least words that anyone would recognize.

"I'm sorry, Dad," I said. "I guess I'm a real loser at Scrabble."

My father was quiet for a long time. I didn't know if he was mad or sad or surprised or all of those things.

He stood up and started to put the Scrabble board away. That was not good. I couldn't let him go into the living room to watch TV. I had to keep him away from TV for the whole night.

"I could try again, Dad," I said. "I'll concentrate really hard this time."

My dad smiled at me.

"How about chess, Hank?" he said. "I really feel like a game of chess."

"Wow, so do I!" I said.

I am a whiz at chess.

My dad and I played thirteen games of chess. We played right up until bedtime. I beat him every game except one. He didn't even mind losing. And the best part was, he never even mentioned the TV.

No, that's not true.

The best part was, my dad and I really had fun.

CHAPTER 21

ONE OF THE THINGS my friends and I are very good at is making plans. Take, for instance, the one we made for getting the new cable box installed. We worked on it all during lunch period the next day.

THE MAGIK 3 PLAN FOR SAVING HANK ZIPZER'S BUTT (AGAIN!)

1. TUESDAY, 3:00 SHARP. Come straight home from school. Hank and Ashley report to Hank's apartment to wait for the cable guy.
2. Frankie stands watch for him in front of building. Robert goes to his apartment to wait for orders.
3. When the cable guy arrives at our building, Frankie buzzes Hank's apartment three times, then keeps the cable guy

busy for exactly two minutes and thirty seconds.

4. Ashley calls Robert and tells him to come up right away.
5. Robert arrives at Hank's. Asks Mr. Zipzer to come to his apartment and help him with a crossword puzzle. Tells him it's a vocab emergency.
6. Mr. Zipzer leaves apartment and goes to Robert's. Robert keeps him there for *at least* fifteen minutes. (Don't mess up, Robert!)
7. Hank buzzes downstairs to signal Frankie that the coast is clear. Frankie brings the cable guy up.
8. The cable guy installs the new box.
9. When he leaves, Ashley calls Robert to tell him to release Mr. Zipzer.
10. Ashley, Frankie, and Robert go home for dinner. Hank watches the nightly news with his dad. Hank acts like nothing happened.

Now I ask you, is this a thing of beauty or not?

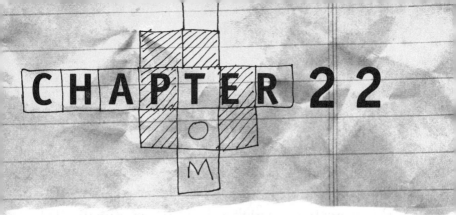

CHAPTER 22

OUR PLAN COULDN'T have started out any better. My dad walked us home from school and we took our positions. Robert went to his apartment. Frankie waited out front. He had a Spaulding high bounce with him, to help him pass the time. Ashley and I went to my apartment and had some cookies and milk. The cookies and milk part wasn't in the plan, but when you're doing battle, you have to eat to keep your energy up.

Emily was out of our hair. She went right into my bedroom to be with Katherine, who was sitting on her nest looking a little more disgusting than usual.

At four fourteen P.M. the buzzer rang.

Bzzzzzz. It only rang once. What was wrong with Frankie? He was supposed to buzz three times.

"Maybe he forgot the signal," Ashley said.

Meanwhile, Cheerio, who believes that buzzer is out to get him, started to bark and chase his tail.

"Calm yourself, boy," I said. I really love Cheerio, but right now, there was no room in this plan for a psycho dog.

Bzzzzz. The buzzer rang again. We waited for the third ring. Instead I heard my neighbor, Mrs. Fink, on the intercom.

"Hankie, sweetheart, I just got back from the skin doctor. I have such a rash, you should see it. Anyway, I forgot my key. Could you buzz me in?"

"Sure, Mrs. Fink. I hope your rash doesn't spread," I said.

I buzzed her in quickly. This is exactly the kind of unexpected event that can make your stomach do flips all over your body. I wondered if George Washington had a lady with a rash bothering him when he was trying to cross the Delaware. I don't think so.

Ashley and I sat down to wait some more.

At four thirty-one, the buzzer rang.

Bzzzz. Bzzzz. Bzzzz. Three rings!

Ashley dialed Robert's number.

"It's a go," she said.

One minute later, Robert was at our door. I was waiting for him.

"He's in the kitchen," I whispered. "And Robert, we're counting on you."

"I've been training for this moment for years," Robert said.

Robert hurried past me and I followed him into the kitchen.

"How ya doin', Mr. Z," he said to my dad. "This is some weather we're having, huh?"

I motioned for Robert to hurry. He had a little part in this. He didn't have to turn it into a starring role.

"Actually, I was wondering if you would mind coming to my apartment for fifteen . . . I mean . . . a few minutes," Robert said. "I have to create a crossword puzzle for school, and I'm stuck. It's really good up to seven down but then I don't know where to go."

I started to cough to cut him off. As a matter of fact, I had a seizure. Robert looked over at me and I told him with my eyes to wrap it up.

"No one knows crossword puzzles like you

do, Mr. Z.," he said. "So could you come help me?"

My dad looked like he had been asked to the wizards' ball. He couldn't have been happier.

"Hank, are you okay if I pop downstairs to Robert's?" he asked.

"I'm fine, Dad. Take your time. Really. It's just great that you're willing to lend this little guy a helping hand."

The minute they were out the door, I pressed the buzzer three times and spoke into the intercom.

"All clear, Frankie," I said.

"It's about time," he said. "I'm running out of conversation with Mr. Cable."

I waited by the elevator door. When it opened, Frankie came out, followed by the cable guy. He had a ponytail and was wearing a blue uniform with his name, TOM, embroidered over his shirt pocket. He was carrying a new cable box in his hand. What a beautiful sight!

"Right this way," I said, showing him into the living room. The moment Cheerio saw Tom, he attacked his ankles and started chewing on his pant legs. In Cheerio language, this is a sign of true love. He only does that to people he really likes, such as Papa Pete.

Tom didn't mind. In fact, he laughed. He reached down to pet Cheerio, and my little dog rolled over on his back for Tom to scratch his stomach. It was a total love fest.

"Sir, I hate to break this up," I said, "but we're kind of in a hurry." I pointed to the cable box in Tom's hand. I was trying not to be rude.

"You kids have money to pay for this?" Tom asked.

Ashley handed him an envelope with cash. We had all pooled our money and I got the last five dollars out of Emily. I had to make a few small threats, but eventually she came through.

"Fifty-eight dollars and forty cents exactly," Ashley said.

Tom took his clipboard and started to write out a receipt. This was eating up valuable time.

"Would it be okay if you start installing the box now?" I asked Tom.

"You guys must be planning to watch something special on the Cartoon Network," he said, as he attached the new cables to the back of our TV. "Personally, I like the old cartoons. That Tweety Bird cracks me up. *I tot I taw a puddy cat.* Yeah, that's great stuff. Now Woody Woodpecker—he's one irritating bird."

Tom seemed like a really nice guy. I would have liked to continue the conversation, but this wasn't the time or place. I didn't trust Robert to keep my father busy for long.

"Now if you'll just give me your old box, I'll be on my way," Tom said when he was finished.

"We don't have an old box," Ashley said.

Tom picked up his clipboard and looked over a sheet of yellow paper on the top. "Says here you do," he answered. "The company wants it back or I have to charge you twenty-five dollars more. Company policy."

"But we don't have any more money," I said.

Tom started unscrewing the cable box.

"Wait," I said. "Listen, Tom, you seem like a nice guy. Can I trust you with a secret?"

"Depends," he said.

I motioned for him to follow me. I led him to the door of my room. Emily was sitting on the floor next to Katherine.

"There's the cable box," I said. "My sister's

pet iguana laid eggs in it. If you take it now, you'll be interrupting the life cycle of forty-five adorable baby iguanas waiting to be born. You wouldn't want to do that, would you?"

"Heck, no!" said Tom. "Did you know you're talking to a charter member of the S.P.P.I.?"

"I had no idea," I answered. "What's the S.P.P.I.?"

"The Society for the Protection and Preservation of Iguanas," he said. "I've been raising iggies since I was your age."

Frankie, Ashley, and I almost fainted. This was too good to be true.

"Do you mind if I have a look at your iggie?" Tom said.

"Watch out," I warned. "She's in a nasty mood."

"You would be too if you just laid forty-five eggs," Emily said.

Tom scooted over next to Katherine, and started talking to her in a soft voice. "Hi, sugar," he said. "You're a good iggie." Slowly, he edged closer and closer to her. The funny thing is, Katherine didn't hiss at him. In fact, she kind of closed her eyes like she was falling asleep. Tom touched her head, and stroked her along the side of her belly. Then gently, he picked her up off the nest.

"Just as I thought," he whispered. "Take a look."

We looked down into Katherine's nest. We saw my father's underpants, and mine, too. We saw the cotton balls and the toilet paper and my mom's slipper. But there wasn't an egg to be seen. Not one.

"There's nothing in there!" Emily said.

"Exactly," Tom said.

"Katherine, girlfriend, you are one big fake," Frankie said.

"You mean she wasn't even pregnant?" asked Emily.

"Oh she was pregnant, all right," said Tom. "Two or three months ago."

Three months ago! That was when we went to Niagara Falls and left Katherine at Pets for U and Me. This was starting to make sense!

"You see," Tom went on, "iguanas don't sit on their eggs. After they lay them, they leave and go somewhere soft and comfortable to recover."

"Like to a cable box with underwear in it?" I said.

"Exactly," Tom answered. "She was just resting up in there from the hard work of laying her eggs."

"But if the eggs aren't in there, then where are they?" Ashley asked.

"Good question," Tom said. "She's hidden them around here somewhere."

My stomach did a triple flip this time. Maybe we accidentally fried her eggs and ate them for breakfast. Or maybe they were in my toothbrush and I swallowed them when I rinsed. Eeeeuuuuuwww. I hope not. Maybe . . .

My thoughts were interrupted by a sound I didn't like. It was footsteps, coming into our apartment, down the hall, and into my room. I looked up.

"Dad!" I said in a shocked voice. "What are you doing here?"

CHAPTER 23

MY FATHER LOOKED AROUND, and I can tell you this, he didn't like what he saw. And that just might be the understatement of the century.

"Who are you?" he said to Tom.

"I'm the cable guy, sir," said Tom.

"He's also a charter member of the Society for the Protection and Preservation of Iguanas," said Emily.

"I'm sure that's a very worthy organization," said my father, turning to Tom, "but may I ask why you are in my apartment?"

"Actually, we called him," said Robert, who had just come panting into the room.

"Robert," I said. "You were supposed to keep my dad away for fifteen minutes."

"I couldn't help it," said Robert. "He came back for his mechanical pencil. He said he can't do crosswords without it."

Why hadn't I thought of that? Of course. His mechanical pencil!

"Hank, you have a lot of explaining to do," said my father.

"Maybe I should be going," Tom said.

"That's a good idea," answered my father. "Hank, come with me." He turned to Tom. "What do I owe you for the service call?"

"Nothing," answered Tom. "The kids took care of it."

My father nodded and walked into the living room. I followed him.

"What's the meaning of this?" he said.

"I'm going to explain everything, Dad. I promise. You remember when we had that nice talk about Thomas Edison and what a cool inventor he was?"

"Cut to the chase, Hank," my father said.

"Well, young Thomas must have taken apart plenty of things before he invented the light-bulb. And I bet he couldn't put all of them back together, either."

"Such as a cable box," my dad said.

"Good, Dad. You're following right along. That's excellent."

Out of the corner of my eye, I saw Tom making his way to the front door. He probably thought he had wandered into a family of lunatics.

"So you called the cable company to replace the box you broke," my dad said. "And I assume you weren't planning on telling me any of this."

"Excellent, Dad. I admire your problem-solving skills."

My dad was so mad his eyes were spinning around in his head, like those guys who slam into mountains in Road Runner cartoons.

"Actually, we could have fixed it, Mr. Z, but then Katherine laid eggs in it," Robert said. He and the others had joined me in the living room—for moral support, I guess.

"That is, we thought she laid eggs in it," Ashley said.

"Turns out, she laid them somewhere else," Emily said.

"We just don't know where," Frankie added.

"Now we do." It was Tom, bent over the potted palm tree next to the front door of our apartment. "Here they are!"

We all bolted over to take a look. A clump of soft brownish eggs was half buried in the dirt around the tree. There weren't forty-five of them, but there were a lot.

"Look, Dad," I whispered. "Katherine's babies."

"Hank, if you think this is going to get you out of the hot water you're in, you have a lot to learn, young man."

"Excuse me, sir," whispered Tom. "The first one is being born. Maybe you'd like to watch."

We gathered around. It was truly unbelievable. A tiny iguana was chewing his way out one of the eggs. We saw his snout first and then out popped his little face. He blinked and looked around. He seemed to be looking right at me. I couldn't believe that I was the first face he ever saw.

"Hi, little guy," I said. He was so cute. He was more than cute. He was spectacular.

"This is a miracle," Emily said. She had tears in her eyes.

We all did. Even me.

CHAPTER 24

Go to next page.
→

SIX THINGS I TOLD MY DAD YOU SHOULDN'T TALK ABOUT DURING THE MIRACLE OF IGUANA BIRTH

1. Cable boxes or anything having to do with them.
2. Punishments, or anything having to do with them.
3. Anything having to do with anything other than iguana birth.
4.
5.
6.

You know what? I can't concentrate on this list right now. There are baby iguanas being born as I write this. It is so exciting, I don't even understand why you're reading this list. Trust me. Hurry up and skip to the next chapter.

CHAPTER 25

KATHERINE LAID TWENTY-THREE eggs in all. We sat around in a semicircle that we made with our dining room chairs and watched as nineteen iguanas hatched that night. Nineteen tiny little lizards poking their snouts into the world. I wish you could have been there.

I guess the last four weren't in such a hurry to come into the world. They must have been so comfortable inside their eggs. All warm and snuggly. Maybe their cable boxes were working, and they were just waiting for their favorite show to end.

My mom came home from the deli in time to see all but the first two being born. She wanted to name every single one of them Spencer, which is what she wanted to name me before I was born only my dad wouldn't let her. She invited Tom to stay for dinner. It turns out he's not only an iggie expert but also a vegetarian who really loved her cauliflower casserole with mock tuna. It's a good thing he ate it, because the rest of us were looking for a place to toss it. Even Cheerio turned up his nose at it.

My dad did take me into my room for "the talk," in between when Dexter and Barbara were born. He told me that I was going to have to pay back everyone for the cable box, but he didn't ground me. He went easy on me because although I made a mistake, I did it in the name of science.

Ashley, Frankie, and Robert had to go home after the first nineteen were born. It was almost midnight, and we had school the next day. My dad went to bed too, and took Emily's guide book on *Raising Your Iguana* with him. I don't know why he was reading it now—we had already given birth to nineteen healthy reptiles. What more did you need to know?

Emily had fallen asleep in my mom's lap. Maybe it was the miracle of birth that was making me feel all gooey, but she looked very sweet.

Tom and I sat by the potted palm tree. We just watched in silence for a while as one of the four remaining eggs started to roll around a little.

"Here comes another one," Tom said. "Shouldn't be long now."

"Should I wake Emily up?"

"Let her sleep," whispered my mom. I guess once you've seen nineteen iguanas born, the twentieth is pretty much . . . like . . . you know . . . the nineteenth. Or the eighteenth, for that matter.

We watched in silence some more. The iguana's snout was showing itself, but he was taking a rest before busting all the way out of the egg. It's hard work, getting born.

"So tell me, Hank," Tom said. "Why did you take the cable box apart in the first place?"

I told him the whole story about how I tried to tape the movie for Frankie and how I screwed up.

"What movie was it?" he asked.

"*The Mutant Moth That Ate Toledo.*"

"Oh man, that's a classic," he said.

"So they say," I said. "It's not out on video, and they only play it on TV once a year. My best friend has been waiting to see it his whole life. Now he'll have to wait three hundred and sixty-three more days, thanks to me."

"Hank, look at me," Tom said. "What do you see?"

"A guy." I shrugged.

"A guy who what?"

"A guy who knows a lot about iguanas," I said.

"And?"

"And who works for a cable company."

"Bingo," said Tom. "Hank, I am a cable guy. We carried *The Mutant Moth That Ate Toledo* on our system. Which means I can get you a tape."

I jumped out of my seat, almost out of my skin.

"That is unbelievable," I screamed. I shouted so loud that I scared the little iguana back into its egg.

"Sorry, fella," I said, "but you don't know how exciting this is." I went back to my whispering voice. "You can really get me a copy?"

"Sure," Tom said.

"But I can't pay you," I said. "I only get four dollars and fifty cents a week allowance, and I have to pay everyone back for the new cable box."

"I have a better idea," Tom said. "I'll make you a trade."

"What do I have that you would want?" I said. I thought about it. "Oh, I do have a triple size cat's-eye marble. That's pretty cool."

Tom looked down at the little iguana popping out of the egg. "I wouldn't mind having him."

"Would that be okay, Mom?" I asked.

"It certainly would be," she answered. "We have twenty-two other iguanas to find homes for. I think little Spencer there would be happy to go with Tom."

"Actually, Mrs. Zipzer, I was thinking of naming him Sylvester," said Tom.

I got a washcloth from the bathroom to wrap little Sylvester up in so he'd be comfortable on the way to his new home. It was a Spider-Man washcloth, which I thought Sylvester would like. Tom picked him up and wrapped him gently in it. That little iggie seemed happy as a bug in a rug.

Sylvester was going to get the best home an iguana could have. And I was going to get a personal copy of the best horror movie ever made.

A mutant moth for a baby iguana. That's what I call a good trade.

CHAPTER 26

TOM BROUGHT ME THE TAPE, and I invited Frankie to sleep over on the weekend. I didn't mention the movie.

I was so excited! I could hardly wait for Saturday night. I put the tape in a secret place to make sure Frankie didn't see it. I hid it in my third drawer, under my Mets sweatshirt. Then I got worried that I'd forget where the secret place was, so I wrote notes to myself on Post-Its. But I had to write them in code so Frankie wouldn't figure out what I'd planned for him.

I drew a baseball bat and wrote "Mets Rule" on all the notes. I put one on my clock radio, and one on the mirror in the bathroom, and one on the chart above my desk. When Frankie came over, he looked around and said, "What's with all the Mets stuff?"

"They're reminders," I said.

"Of what? That the Mets suck?"

"No, of where I hid . . ."

"Hid what?" Frankie wanted to know.

I bit my lip really hard. That secret wanted to come out so bad. I was dying to tell him, but that would ruin the surprise.

Somehow, I made it until Saturday. My parents were going out and Papa Pete was staying with us. He and I put together a great plan.

We set up sleeping bags in the living room, right in front of the TV. Emily was in her room making little cots out of construction paper and toothpicks for all twenty-two baby iguanas. She had come up with a way to make pillows out of cotton balls. That would keep her busy all night. Besides, horror movies were not her cup of chocolate milk.

When Frankie got there, Papa Pete made us pastrami sandwiches with brown mustard on seedless rye. Put a crunchy pickle next to that and you can't beat it.

After dinner, it was time for the main event.

"You boys get comfortable in your sleeping bags, and I'll put on a movie," Papa Pete said. "I picked out something that I'm comfortable with you watching while I'm on duty." He winked at me.

He handed me a videotape box. I slid the tape out, and handed the cover to Frankie.

"*The Parent Trap?*" Frankie said. "You've got to be kidding me!"

It was all I could do to keep from bursting out laughing.

"Try it," Papa Pete said.

"I'll hate it," groaned Frankie.

"For years, I wouldn't eat raisins," said Papa Pete. "I thought anything that looks that bad has got to taste bad, too. Then one day, I put some on my cereal. And now, I wouldn't think of starting my day without them."

"Papa Pete," said Frankie. "That's raisins. We're talking about a movie that eight-year-old girls love. How can you compare the two?"

"I watched *The Parent Trap* with Emily a couple weeks ago," I said, trying as hard as I could to keep a straight face. "The part where the parents kiss is pretty interesting."

"Zip, I think your brains have fallen out and turned into marshmallows," Frankie said.

"Just put the tape in," said Papa Pete. "No

violence, no naked ladies, good family fun."

"I'm going to be sick," Frankie said. "Correction. I *am* sick."

"Enjoy yourselves, gentlemen," Papa Pete said and he went into the kitchen.

I couldn't look at Frankie. Slowly, I moved my finger toward the PLAY button and pressed it. Then I hurled myself across the room onto my sleeping bag. I tried to watch the screen, but I kept one eye on Frankie to see his reaction.

The music came up and the picture came on. It was a deserted cabin in the wilderness. A window was broken and the night was dark. Too dark.

"Hey, this doesn't look like *The Parent Trap*," Frankie said.

All of a sudden, a giant moth came flying out of the shattered window of the cabin and filled the screen. Its eyes glowed red. It spread its wings and the title came up across them. THE MUTANT MOTH THAT ATE TOLEDO.

Frankie sat straight up in his sleeping bag.

"No way!" he said. "No way!"

This was truly one of the happiest moments of my life.

"Zip!" Frankie said. He was so excited he couldn't even put together a sentence. "You . . . moth . . . here . . . now . . . No way! NO WAY!"

Papa Pete had opened the kitchen door a slice. He was smiling. I was smiling. Frankie was smiling.

"How did you do this, Zipola?" Frankie asked.

"I made a promise to you, and I messed up. I had to fix it."

"Well, you can mess up as much as you want if this is the way it ends up," Frankie said. "This is so cool I don't know what to say!"

"That's good," I said. "Because you're not supposed to talk during a movie."

Papa Pete pushed the door all the way open and brought in a bowl filled with an assortment of ice cream bars. He sat down on the couch and the three of us spent the next two hours screaming our heads off, enjoying *The Mutant Moth That Ate Toledo*.

CHAPTER 27

THERE'S A LESSON IN THIS STORY, which is: you never know where a great science project is going to come from. You start off with the tummy sliding habits of penguins. Then you're discovering the wonders inside the cable box. And you wind up observing and recording the reproductive cycle of the apartment-dwelling iguana in modern day Manhattan.

My science project turned out great. Thank goodness my disposable camera still had 27 shots left from our trip to Niagara Falls. I got some really good pictures of those eensy teensy iguanas eating their way out of their eggs.

I would've gotten an A on it. I was so close I could taste it. But Ms. Adolf took points off because of my concluding sentence. It said: "I think baby iguanas are the most lovable creatures in the world." Ms. Adolf didn't think that

152

was scientific enough.

I got a B, though, which is great for me. I don't get a lot of Bs. The really important thing is I got an A in friendship. Frankie and I are back to being best friends—better than ever.

Hey, you. Baby Iguana Head! What do you think you're doing?

Listen, I've got to go. One of the twenty-two baby iguanas has gotten in my drawer. I think it's Max. Or it could be Sneezy. Or maybe it's Charlotte. It's so hard to tell the difference.

Oh no you don't, whoever you are! You poop on my Mets sweatshirt and I'm telling your mom!

Hey, I've got to take care of this. I'll see you all later.

About the Authors

HENRY WINKLER is an actor, producer, and director and he speaks publicly all over the world. Holy mackerel! No wonder he needs a nap. He lives in Los Angeles with his wife, Stacey. They have three children named Jed, Zoe, and Max and two dogs named Monty and Charlotte. If you gave him one word to describe how he feels about this book, he would say, "Proud."

If you gave him two words, he would say, "I am so happy that I got a chance to write this book with Lin and I really hope you enjoy it." That's twenty-two words, but hey, he's got learning challenges.

LIN OLIVER is a writer and producer of movies, books and television series for children and families. She has created over one hundred episodes of television, four movies and seven books. She lives in Los Angeles with her husband, Alan. They have three sons named Theo, Ollie, and Cole, one fluffy dog named Annie, and no iguanas.

If you gave her two words to describe this book, she would say, "funny and compassionate." If you asked her what compassionate meant, she would say, "full of kindness." She would not make you look it up in the dictionary.